Charles R. Ashbee

A Few Chapters in Workshop Re-Construction and Citizenship

Charles R. Ashbee

A Few Chapters in Workshop Re-Construction and Citizenship

ISBN/EAN: 9783337405922

Printed in Europe, USA, Canada, Australia, Japan

Cover: Foto ©Andreas Hilbeck / pixelio.de

More available books at **www.hansebooks.com**

CHAPTERS IN WORKSHOP RE-CONSTRUCTION AND CITIZEN-SHIP.

A FEW CHAPTERS IN WORK-SHOP RE-CONSTRUCTION AND CITIZENSHIP, BY C. R. ASHBEE, M.A., ARCHITECT, KING'S COLLEGE, CAMBRIDGE.

PUBLISHED BY THE GUILD AND SCHOOL OF HANDICRAFT, ESSEX HOUSE, MILE END ROAD, LONDON.
1894.

To the memory of C. W. Atkinson, Guildsman, and First Apprentice in the Guild of Handicraft ; in whom many hopes for the New Citizenship were centred, whose loving comradeship inspired much of the confidence of these chapters, but who died suddenly as their last words were being prepared for press, June 4. 1894, age 20.

CONTENTS.

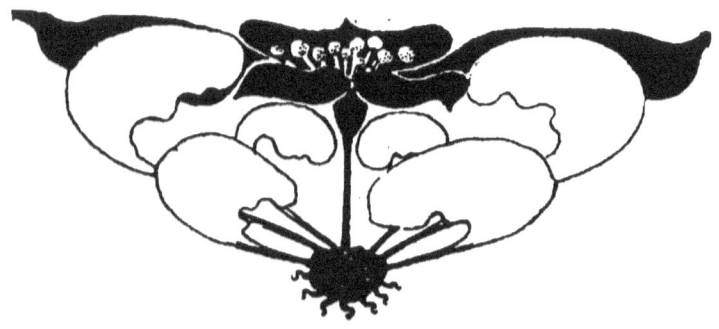

CONTENTS—*continued*.

 *Many of the following Chapters have been written as they have been called for, at different times during the last six years; and they have served, in most cases, to illustrate some workshop endeavour or some educational principle.*

The fact that they spring from the various moments of experience in a busy life, must be the excuse for thus offering them in almost fragmentary form.

CHAPTER I.—A FEW DE-
FINITIONS TOWARDS AN
IDEAL.

We have reached a stage in our social development when
it behoves us to ask what is to be our Ideal of Citizenship ?
How far are we to look for the formation of the citizen in
our modern system of industry—the workshop—how far in
education provided by the State ? What is to be the interaction of these two generative forces ? and what are to be
the limitations of individuality, whether permitted or
encouraged, in either case ?

When we ask the average Englishman, no matter from
what class he be drawn, what he means by "a gentleman,"
we find him offering a variety of different enterpretations,
each differently qualified. It is the "fine old English
Gentleman," or "Gentleman of the Guards" over a glass of
port wine, or "Mr. Chairman and Gentlemen" at a
Trafalgar Square meeting ; the word has lost its standard
quality. We are apt to forget how recent has been this
change. The old Renaissance Ideal, based upon the
Cortegiano of Italy, and which was stamped upon the
English character by the personality of Sir Philip Sidney,
lasted well into this century. That Ideal implied character
and behaviour qualified by blood. But it was found in-
sufficient in a commercial century, and after Napoleon had
preached "la carrière ouverte aux talents," to meet what
was wanted, and so we have the "self-made man," who,
under certain conditions, is also permitted to rank as a
"gentleman." In him something else takes the place of
"blood," and we have character and behaviour qualified by
"energy" or "organising capacity," or some other domi-
nating force applicable to the time with which he is striving.
But the second Ideal bids fair to have shorter sway than the
first, we are already searching about for another. Who is
to be the gentleman of the newer time, and what is to be
his measure ? We need not trouble ourselves about the
word "gentleman," but we need the object, we need the
standard. Character and behaviour must be there, but
qualified by what ? In this lies our problem of the Ideal of
Citizenship.

I shall try in the following chapters to offer a few
practical suggestions, if I may be allowed to call them so,

The re-construction of the workshop and the traning of the citizen drawn from personal experience in certain branches of work on the shaping of this ideal? They deal broadly with two large questions—the *Re-construction of the Workshop* and the *Training of the Citizen for the Workshop*, and if my own point of view is necessarily a limited one and the criticism be offered that England's greater industrialism, or larger problems of education cannot be judged or guided from it, I can only answer that though I admit the validity of the criticism, I do not consider that it goes far. No one should speak on educational matters unless he has himself had experience in education; no one should speak, much less generalize, in the problems of Industry unless he has, in some measure, lived through the details of a workshop. Though the application of some of the suggestions in the following chapters—suggestions on industrial partnership, artistic and technical training, the scope of the decorative arts, systems of industrial teaching through apprenticeship, or through University Extension, the limitations of personality in Industry, and the freeing of personality in education would each need qualifying in their special bearing on every case, I venture to think that generalization, from my own limited point of view, may none the less be permissible, and that it may even serve as a guide for construction in other lines of Industry to which it has no direct reference. The industrial organization of the mine, the mill, and the dockyard, must always remain quite a different thing from that of the builder's yard, the cabinet maker's, jeweller's, or blacksmith's shop, or any form of production in which the hand and its individuality may prevail over the machine, but I believe that object lessons from the re-construction of the latter, may also be drawn for the use of the former. They do not, however, come within the scope of these essays.

Art, craft, and industry. It will be needful, however, at starting, since the words Art, Craft, and Industry, play a prominent part through the book, to offer some definition of them, at least in so far as they are used in contradistinction to each other. I imply by the three terms, then, broadly the following: by Art the highest imaginative production for human delight or service, and I am content to accept the definition of Ruskin that the object of Art is either to tell a true thing or to adorn a serviceable one, whether in a nocturne of Whistler, a jewel of Cellini, or a cretonne of Morris. By craft, technical production, in which the hand works alone or under the immediate guidance of the brain, the same three illustrations

10

serving here if we divest them of their creative origin. By Industry, production in which the machine or the hand works, but not under the direct guidance of the brain, the cretonne again, when it is being stamped, or the various portions of the Cellini jewel when it is being reproduced by the mechanical processes of modern Birmingham. It will be seen at once that these definitions are very superficial, and that they overlap each other. The difference between the three words is, however, rather one of degree, and one could trace the chain of production, link by link, downwards from a picture of Burne-Jones, through a chair of Chippendale to the phosphor tip of the lucifer produced by the Bow match-girl and her attendant machines.

We are all very weary of talking about Art, and since there is much talk about Art in the following chapters, let me say at once that it is not my wish to preach Beauty, or in any way to make it an object at which to aim. Beauty is only harmony of structure, and therefore a result. I am quite content to let it find its own way to the light, all I assert is that if in any way it is to be made an element in our productions, or in the life of our citizens, we must first re-construct the workshop, that is to say, our system of production in its social and industrial bearings, and re-model our standard of education, that is to say, the pattern or mould of our future citizens. To say we are not an artistic nation is to beg the question. No nation is artistic when its interests are absorbed in other things that, for the time, appear to be more important—for instance, war, religious disputation, commerce. Art does not run in nations so much as in individuals, and it expresses itself in character in direct relation to the community's desire for it, to the leisure and opportunity given it. In the terms of the economist, it is a matter of supply and demand. One of the objects of these essays is to show, not that the demand should be created and the supply increased, but that the demand is already there, only misdirected, and the supply produced on false and artificial systems, in part because of this misdirected demand. That in fine, what we have to do is to guide demand by education and to influence supply by workshop re-construction.

And what is our artistic standard to be? The public hall, the west-end drawing-room, the suburban parlour, the shop front, the commercial article, we believe that they are not somehow as good as they might be; how are we to judge them, how know when a thing is to be approved? Shall we

The province of beauty in social development

The producer himself the standard

take the advertisement on the outside of the pill-box? or believe the honied words of the bagman? or be dazzled by the fashionable acclamations at an academy soirée? or the concensus of public opinion thundered forth by a democratic press? I answer, the artistic standard is the artist, the productive standard the producer. Whether he work in his studio in Holland Park, or in his sweating den in White-chapel, it is to the artist, the producer, that we must look, he is the ultimate unit in whom and in whose life lies the determination of the standard, he has the standard within him.

It is well that in our constructive citizenship we should bear this constantly in mind. Let us remember it when we hold in our hands anything made to-day for our service. " The commercial article," for instance, made not to use but to sell. Let us ask ourselves where was the producer, and what manner of man was he? It is well that we should bear this in mind when we walk these streets of London. Every now and then through this wilderness of brick and stone we come upon a reminiscence of other happier conditions, but only in name, for looking to the corners of the nearest brickwork, or asking some inhabitant, we mock-ingly learn that it is Bethnal Green, or Hackney Downs, Bow Common, Cambridge Heath, Mile End Waste or Stepney Green: a whiff of the fresh fields of a hundred years ago comes back to us. Let us remember, then, that sweeter conditions of life are an essential to better production.

The move ment for re-con-struction and the movement for hu-manism None of the themes in the following chapters lay claim to novelty in themselves. To the founder of Christianity, to the Athenian Citizen, to the mediæval state builders, and to the modern exponents of socialistic economics, they might all be traced, but my effort has been to point to a few newer applications and to make clearer, positions often misunderstood by thoughtful men, whose experience and sympathies lie elsewhere. I believe that there are two movements going on in our midst which are tending to the expression of the new citizenship, and they are the *Re-con-struction of the Workshop* and the *humanising of the citizen*. I would ask for a closer study of the former and a more generous encouragement of the latter. In the former we have, on the part of the workman, the producer, an unconscious reversion to the mediæval state, the central idea of which was the maintenance of a moral code and an economic standard of life conformably with it. In the latter, we have through the educationalist, and the citizen

12

himself, a readiness to enter again into that culture as it was understood by the great thinkers, poets and painters of the 15th and 16th centuries—we have, potentially, the spirit of the Renaissance.

The wave of revolutionary socialism that broke over us in the years 1880-90, has spent its force, done its work, and the result has been a variety of efforts in social re-construction throughout the country, and a strengthening and amplifying, owing to the new impulse, of older institutions already in existence. The points of view of the constructive and the revolutionary socialist, are, as I understand them, much the same, only the former makes for his end the re-construction of society by little pieces of work here and there; while the latter says, it is no use tinkering, we must clear the old society away first before we can reconstruct the new. English love of order and constitutionalism will inevitably, indeed has already, given judgment in favour of the former, and we find the collectivist ideal, if not accepted, certainly compromised with, and often acted upon in every department of the State, whether under the guidance of the so-called Conservative or the so-called Liberal. The socialistic propaganda has, in other words, bitten into modern English political philosophy until we conceive it within the bounds of possibility that a Conservative Government shall, some day, give us land nationalization, even as it has given us factory acts and free education. [Revolutionary and constitutional socialism]

But apart from its political or semi-political aspects, the new thought has an due influence and is daily exerting a greater influence upon life, upon our relations towards one another, upon our way of regarding labour, upon the morale that underlies our conduct either in individual or collective citizenship. [The new morale of labour]

In the little world of Art, or as I would prefer to put it, of the *higher production*, this might be illustrated by the number of men and women who have suddenly awakened to the fact that there are other things in Art besides the laying on of oil paints upon canvas, their standard of life is not deteriorating because of this, indeed they find that life is becoming more real, more genuine. At the same time the greater underlying workmen's movement of the raising of the standard of life is going on quite apart from this and working out its own destinies. The former is but a trifle compared in magnitude to the latter, but if, as is most probable, the two are destined soon to consolidate, the former may help to leaven the latter. It is by the filtering down of the cultured middle and upper class, who are taking up forms of production as a duty, a necessity or a pastime, that what is foolishly called "bringing Art to the masses" will be effected; not by picture exhibitions in the East End, not by fashionable performances at charities. The artifical social barrier that divides the "gentleman" who has taken up painting, bookbinding, metal work, or pottery, from the journey-man bookbinder, potter, coppersmith, or carpenter, cannot last long, in the end both must be judged by the goodness or beauty of the work of their hands.

Indeed, one might almost say that the social code with regard to labour had changed much in the last two decades, and not only is the man of no occupation, whatever his dependence on society, beginning to be looked upon as a doubtful model, but more dignity is daily being accorded to those that labour either with brain or hand. If a young man dawdles along Kensington with an empty barrow and a spade chanting a melancholy dirge, or goes from house to house in exquisite kid gloves making afternoon calls, the feeling of contemptuous pity with which he is regarded is much the same in each case, and the right minded Englishman says of him, "Oh, the poor devil's got no work to do!"

What in our social development, then, we appear, whether consciously or not, to be tending towards, is a state governed and guided by its producers. It is no small question, therefore, for those of us who are dealing with education or with the higher forms of production, to consider what manner of men these producers are to be, and what manner of things they are to produce. "By the work of their hands ye shall know them." But what is to be the standard of this work of their hands, how far is it to be a part of their life, and affect the formation of their character as men; and, above all, how are we, the State and those who are doing its educational work, to lay a firm and wise foundation for the training of the young producer, the future citizen? How are we to shape our Ideal of Citizenship?

CHAPTER 2. — ON THE NEED FOR THE CULTIVATION OF THE SENSE OF BEAUTY, AND THE QUESTIONABLE WISDOM OF HOPING FOR THIS FROM THE BRITISH MIDDLE CLASS.

In the last chapter I said that my intention was not to preach Beauty. To offer a chapter, therefore, on the need for the cultivation of the sense of Beauty might appear paradoxical. Let me repeat then my qualifying data. If Beauty is to be made an element in our productions or in the life of our citizens we must first re-construct the workshop and re-model the standard of their education, that is to say, cultivate the sense within them.

By this sense I mean *the power of wisely using and enjoying natural surroundings and the human body, and a second similar power in the work of human creation—a noble building, a great picture, a refined piece of handicraft, national poetry and music.*

By the cultivation of this sense I mean the relating it to our daily life as individuals and as a community, and giving it thereby that truer proportion towards the other things that we enjoy, such as reading newspapers, betting at horse races, going to church in smart clothes, or gossiping at afternoon teas ; and the training of our children to this end by a fundamental understanding of colour, line, form, mass, music, natural surroundings and the enjoyments of the human body. By the British middle class, I mean that vulgar lump to which we all belong, from the superior artisan, who is just beginning to think better of working with his hands, upwards indefinitely, and inclusive of the average tradesman, parson, professional man, Royal Academician, or nonchalant aristocrat. They whose habitations are somewhat grimly prim, who delight in having what all the other commonplace people have, and in doing what all the other commonplace people do. To hope for the cultivation of the sense of Beauty from these people is a matter of questionable wisdom.

A few aphorisms I would like in this chapter to offer a few aphorisms that may guide us in thinking over our problems of workshop re-construction, and these are they. I would lay it down :

That the crown and fulfilment of national life is a wise understanding and enjoyment of Beauty.

That the only hope for the development of the sense of Beauty is among the artificially cultured class of artists and the artisan ; the one conscious, the other unconscious.

That under modern conditions of Art, picture painting is forced into an artificial prominence and the constructional and decorative arts, the real backbone, have, as yet, no right recognition among us.

That the problems of machine production will have by degrees to be solved from within the workshop. That a sharp distinction will have to be drawn between what is produced by machinery and the direct work of man's hands, and that the standard of artistic excellence must depend ultimately upon the pleasure given, not to the consumer, but to the producer.

That at the present day the social problem has prior claim to the artistic.

Beauty as fulfilment I begin by postulating that the crown and fulfilment of national life is a wise understanding and enjoyment of Beauty. The perfected citizen should have the power of which I spoke above, and upon the modern man we have yet to graft the purity of Hellas and the spirit of the Renaissance. Though I do not put reverence for Beauty as necessarily the first thing for each man's individual observance, I put it very high, and I certainly place it first, and as above, and containing all other things for the observance of the community. A national reverence for Beauty is the greatest of the great things a nation can possess. Rome may have been great for Cæsar and Justinian, but Greece was greater for Sophocles and Pheidias. England may be great for Clive, Wellington, Stevenson and Peel, but future times will hold her greater for Shakespeare, Antonio More, John Thorpe, and William of Wykeham. Florence means to us the great life of the fifteenth century, Granada the refined civilization of the Moors. If we look, we find that all great historical association implies some fundamental reverence for the sense of Beauty as the quality by which a community's greatness endures.

Then as to the average Englishman of to-day, does he
possess this quality in himself, and do we, as a Community, delight in it? I think not. We look around and see it absent. The artisan lives a dull and indifferent life, his absorbing thought is the social question; the professional man, well, he ministers to the lives of the other uninteresting people, for as a community having an appreciation for Beauty, we nineteenth century English are an uninteresting people at home. We may be very strong and look very big abroad, but at home we are not interesting, our commercialism has made us lose sight of the right proportions of life. See those splendid men, our lawyers, they are good types of Englishmen, look at them in the National Portrait Gallery, whole rows of them, square foreheads, bridged noses, heavy underhanging chins, coarse old fellows all of them, we cannot expect much understanding of Beauty from them, yet their interpretation and way of looking at it as expressed some while since in the Whistler trial, for instance, is shared by the average British Philistine.

" How long did it take you to knock off that Nocturne ? " asks the lawyer of the painter.

" Two hours."

" Isn't £200 rather a stiffish price for two hours' work ? "

To which the answer naturally is that the price was for the study of a life-time.

We are steeped in the commercial spirit all of us, and we have but one meting rod for all things—" Will it pay ? " Yet by no conceivable means can Beauty be made to pay in the Englishman's sense of the word, and a time may come when some Morgiana will wipe the grease off the rod to which the golden coin sticks.

My friend, the Rev. Simeon Flux, preaches a veritable gospel of Beauty. But, somehow, it does not touch the inner
life of Great Fadwell East. To do him justice, good man, he does his best. He admits that his church is but a specimen of contractor's Gothic, executed thirty years ago under the superintendence of an eminent Ecclesiastical architect, but, somehow, the style, if so it may be called—some Rickman has yet to find its true name, middle Victorian, florid specification, office Flamboyant, what you will—has got lamentably behind the times already. Yet the Rev. Simeon does his best to keep St. Saviour's up to date. His flock's salvation, however, seems always slipping through his fingers. His cure of twenty thousand souls ever appears to be finding its own salvation in spite of him. He does his best. He makes St. Saviour's look, as he says, cheerful, like a drawing-room, but

17

yet it does not entice. He goes to Italy and brings back photographs of Michael Angelos and Francias to hang on the columns of the nave, but to little purpose. He keeps his name and that of his flock before the public by writing letters to the *Times* for books, blankets, subscriptions, according to the season—they take the blankets, but not the Beauty. He orders a big green dossal from a firm of ecclesiastical *entrepreneurs*, and a stained glass window to Lord Brewster of Chingford; he summons debates and holds discussions in the schools, and has got the London University Extension Society to give lectures on Greek Art and Flemish painters to try if that will help; and he preaches a fiery sermon to the press representatives and the great ladies of Bayswater, who drive in flocks to his Lenten sermons in the East. The footmen wait outside while the great preacher is pleading for the poor and the sense of Beauty within; but somehow the heart of Great Fadwell is not turned, neither the photographs, nor the dossal, nor the memory of the big drink peer, nor the fashionable sermon, will woo them; they seem to be working out their own destinies in their own way, unknown and misunderstood by the Rev. Simeon Flux. I fear the end will be a sorry one, and in sheer despair he will accept the inevitable bishopric.

My friend Mr. Pushington, the member for South-west Kensington, and the head partner of Messrs. Sky Sign and Co., the great House that weighs like an indigestion upon the world, also goes in for Beauty, and he encourages it by buying many paintings and supporting many picturesque charities, but somehow his efforts also avail but little, and they appear so personal, so individual, so marginal to life. He also does not touch Great Fadwell East. There is not among us, as yet, any conception of a corporate understanding or enjoyment of Beauty, and as to its entering into our national education that is long to seek. To train a child as Pantagruel was trained, or in the manner in which Vittorino da Feltre sought to bring up the young Gonzage in well balanced grasp of ethics, music, art, languages, history, and athletics seems to us English, sentimental, unpractical; and what is the result? The sense of Beauty is left out of count, it is not thought of consequence, that the child should have its eye trained to form and colour, mass and line, that it should learn to gauge a beautiful picture, or delight in a noble building. At the present moment (January, 1894) the School Board for London, usually considered one of the leading educational bodies of the Kingdom, is, in mere ignorant wastefulness, pulling down the

18

old palace of Bromley-by-Bow, one of the last remaining Elizabethan houses in London, to clear the site for a new Board School. This building, magnificently constructed, has within it some twenty-five panelled rooms of various dates, beautiful carving in stone and wood, two oak staircases, and some of the finest ceilings of modelled plaster work in England, the arms of James I. with the royal insignia in the state room, and portraits of the heroes of antiquity in panelled plaster, Hector of Troy, Alexander of Greece, and Joshua (Dux!). Surely of some educational value all this work so reverently and thoughtfully put together by the old craftsmen of a more beautiful England! Yet so indifferent are our educational authorities to what might be done with it, that they did not even take the trouble to find out what they had on the site, but jobbed the old palace away to a contractor for £250, who sold the internal fittings to a dealer for £167, who proceeded to make a commercial article out of them by offering one mantelpiece alone to the nation for £100.* When those to whom we entrust the training of our children in the sense of Beauty can do this, what may we expect? It is a case of the green tree and the dry.

Meanwhile the two thousand souls of Great Fadwell East, make shift without it. In the second of my aphorisms I ventured on the assertion that the only hope for the development of the sense of Beauty in modern England lies in the artificially cultured class of artists and in the artisan—the one conscious and the other unconscious. The artisan, if any one at all, is laying the foundation for a new order of things, while the artist, unfortunately for himself, works mainly upon the traditions of bygone times, seeing that there is little or no tradition of his own day wherein to work. Thus the one is making for the future, and the other preserving the past, and, as William Morris has well put it, is handing down the golden chain of Beauty that was dropped in the sixteenth century. I do not say that the artisan has any appreciation of the sense of Beauty, far from it, but I affirm that if we could look for its development anywhere, it is with that portion of the community who are seeking to break its commercial traditions and to construct a newer social order, in which, let us hope, the sense of Beauty may find more room for growth. To the artist of to-day and the society of his environment may we alone reasonably look for its understanding, seeing that to him it is a special study, though this special study is often affected by—what shall I

Cultured artist and uncultured artisan

---

* And subsequently, I understand, sold it back again to the School Board for £150 (June, 1894).

19

call it ?—the conditions of the picture market to the painter, the vulgar comforts of his client to the architect ?

It might be supposed that where one has Art, or, let me say rather, the specialization of one or other small portion of it treated by a part of the community as a profession, there would be some lead, some guide for the average man who is seeking to cultivate the sense of Beauty. But this is not so. The Royal Academy of Art, professedly at the head of the artistic world, is but a body of interesting gentlemen, of good social position to begin with, and most of them able brushmen, united as a trade union of painters. They, many of them, sympathise individually with the unity of Art, but, as a body, they neither care nor trouble themselves about it, nor do they understand. The professional painter is an unhealthy production of modern times engendered by an unholy union between the Royal Academy and the British Public. Instead of a charger at the head of the ranks we have, in the Academy, a gilded coach lumbering on behind. Even, in its own narrow sphere of *painting*, the Royal Academy of *Arts* does not fulfil its purpose. It is the mistake of the average Philistine to 'imagine that it represents the living schools of painting. The Royal Academy rarely recognises a school until it has, so to say, worked itself out. When a school has passed from its stage of speculation and experiment, through that of construction, and is becoming mannered, and when a younger generation is already restlessly turning to a fresher inspiration the Royal Academy gives a grudging recognition to one or two individuals whose social position warrants her acceptance. The Royal Academy is eminently feminine and elderly, she is a charming old lady of exquisite manners, delighting in a powder and patch conservatism, very mean and little in her ways of looking at things, terribly mercenary and addicted to the twin English vices of prurience and godliness, not to be moved except when her mentor, the British Public, shouts admonition down her brazen speaking-trumpet. Then she wakes up with a start, rubs her eyes, and says, '' dear me, yes, yes, to be sure," and makes Mr. Burne-Jones and Mr. Sargent associates, though her own predilection was for Mr. Frith and Mr. Herbert, and then, too, she has qualms, and makes up for the mischief she does in her spring shows by holding exhibitions in the winter of the works of the men whom she neglected when they were alive.

If we could from within, rather than from without, revise the charter of the Royal Academy, so as to generously include the constructional and decorative Arts or, better still, if we were to strike out the architects and the sculptors and give up the dishonest pretence that it is an Academy of *Arts*, when it is really only a limited trade union of painters in oil colours, we should be arriving at a fitter sense of the relative proportion of things, and, at the same time, place an old and dignified institution more abreast with the times. But that is always an irksome and ungracious task. I hold that we have to give full and ungrudging recognition to the decorative and constructional Arts—they are usually called " minor," but I don't know why—and get to understand, as a nation, the unity of Art about which artists talk so much. In the words of Michael Angelo, we must know of only one Art. I believe that nine-tenths of our painters would be better at house decoration, carving, book-binding, metal work and handicraft of various kinds, than at picture painting, and, I think, one of the healthiest movements of the day towards a better understanding of the sense of Beauty is that of the Arts and Crafts. One thing, indeed, seems to me imperative. We must get our Art more in touch with the community, more in line with life. The distinction between being alive and dead was brought home to me once very pointedly. A few years ago the Dockers' Union did me the honour of asking me to design and paint them a banner after the great strike ; at the same time the Royal Academy hung a work of mine on the line. I appreciated between the two favours, and though my friend, Mr. Pushington, the member for S.W. Kensington, considerately refrained from congratulating me on the former, I felt that it was a finer thing to blaze in a silken glory of blue and crimson over a Hyde Park demonstration than to be asphyxiated in the architectural room at Burlington House.

If the Docker delights in a blue banner, that is, indeed, a great thing, and more than the middle class man can be got to do ; I don't know exactly what to call him, perhaps his symbol is the top hat, that phallus of respectability which he worships, what does he do or care for the decorative Arts ? What do we care for them, we in our villas out at Tooting, and St. John's Wood and Hampstead ? we in our three or seven years' leased houses in Gower Street and Marylebone ? we who have no public place where we can meet together as citizens, and who loiter outside the plate glass shop fronts in Oxford Street and Tottenham Court Road ? We have neither care nor thought for them, we waste hours of our day in reading villainously printed newspapers illustrated by reproductions of wonderful ingenuity, whose only claim to Beauty is their shallow realism ; we neither know nor care how the table at which we sit, nor the plate off which we eat, is made, nor do we mind whether it pleases us, much less, whether it pleased the man that made it.

The paint-er and the decor-ative arts   It is, as I have said, to the artificially cultured class of artists and to the unconscious mass, the English workman, who has the problem of re-construction in hand, that we must look for the appreciation of the sense of Beauty. But to the artist with a reservation. I do not mean the painters, but all those whose effort is Creation and who have set some standard of Beauty before them. Many of my best friends are painters, but I have little sympathy with their position of isolated self satisfaction. They can put their very life and soul into their canvases and lock themselves up in their frames. If they do not sell, it is, after all, of only secondary importance ; for their greatest work is not dependent upon their remuneration, and they have the inestimable advantage of being able to work out their own technique. It is not so with us decorative artists, we, who seek to be artists, but not of the paint box alone, and who hold Art to be a larger thing than picture painting. We are angry with, and jealous of, the painters. How can we experiment, why should it be for us to show how much has to be done first in social re-construction. How can we work out our problems of technique without a hundred years of workshop tradition behind us ? why should we be made to dig the trenches of the City for which we would carve the temples and gild the vanes ? That is where enters the tragedy of this century's Art, not to the painters, but to the constructional and decorative artists who see the fundamental need for the re-construction of the workshop before the flower of the Art can be fulfilled. Don't you think it is a tragedy for us to know that the work we are doing should have been done a hundred years ago, and to feel the cunning of our hands wasting in idleness,—the enforced idleness of having to organize ?

The re-lation of the decor-ative arts to the industrial system   Here, then, we come to one of the rock difficulties in our problem of workshop re-construction, the question of the relation of the decorative Arts to the industrial system. So big is this problem, and so many-sided, that I can only hope to throw a side light here and there upon it. But I would refer again to the fourth of the aphorisms with which I started above as a guide in our policy of re-construction.

The problems of machine production will have, by degrees, to be solved from within the workshop. A sharp distinction will have to be drawn between what is produced by machinery and the direct work of man's hands, and the standard of

22

artistic excellence will depend ultimately upon the pleasure it gives, not to the consumer, but to the producer. The whole ethics of industry are involved in this, but the ethics of industry will be determined in the workshop only. The Kingdom of God is within us, and the fundamental principles laid down by the great Teacher which have gone to make so many nations great, will be applied as the ultimate test for their solution. The dignity of labour, the standard of life, the necessity of leisure, the need for curtail-ment of unnecessary and unproductive labour, and of national waste, the province of the machine, its position as the basis of social re-construction, these are all primarily workshop problems, and will, in due course, be settled from within, not without, in fact, are being now settled. They are, many of them, questions that we cannot shirk, but they are, many of them, questions whose consideration we can postpone. Upon them, however, Art depends.

What, for instance, is the relation of machinery to Art? And granted the admission of machinery as the basis of the new society, as doing the dirty work of the community, as taking the place of the Greek slave who made the Art of Athens possible, what should it be? I do not think this is a question we need directly trouble ourselves with. If only we can so organize our industry as to make it unwasteful, and draw a distinction between what of production makes for human life and character, and what not, we can leave its relation to Art to settle itself. When I say we, I mean the general public, Mr. Pushington, Mr. Trudge who works in his factory, the Rev. Simeon Flux, the lawyer, the doctor, the tradesman, their province is life before Art, but not so the artist, whose study is Art. I hold it a moral duty in him, a duty he owes to his Art, to take the machine problem into direct consideration. "This frame of mine, this bit of carving, this iron rail, does it bear upon it evidence of having been made with pleasure by the man that made it? has it any individuality? if it has none, then I'll none of it." That is the mental attitude in which the artist should study everything that bears upon his Art.

I know it is difficult, especially for the architect, who strives to be a conscientious artist, and deals with many minutiæ of handicraft; often it is impossible for him to get his information first hand, still more often is it im-possible for him to pay the price demanded for individuality and pleasurable work, but there are means offered to every man who goes to work with singleness of purpose, and these means it is the duty of the artist who, before all other things, aims at the expression of individuality, to seek. I do not say that everything produced without pleasure will, in the end, be useless, but that its ultimate utility to the community will be regulated by the pleasure of its production to the individual, and if it professes to be a work of art, *i.e.*, "to tell a true thing or adorn a serviceable one," it must bear on it the stamp of human individuality that betokens pleasure of production.

Ethics of Production and consumption

We may, therefore, in our reconstructive efforts, set aside the commercial traveller's plea that it is the market, the consumer, that must determine what shall be produced. In the future it will be the producer that will determine. Producer and consumer—that blessed word "mesopotamia!" and will the economist forgive me ?—they are an odd couple, these two, and I like to give them concrete entities. They are kin to the two Welsh dragons in the Mabinogion, who are always trying to eat each other up. Latterly the consumer has had the best of it, but we have got to make him disgorge. We have humoured him, cuddled, spoiled and pampered him, till he has become a wasteful, thriftless, selfish sybarite, whether in Bayswater or in Whitechapel. We have pampered him up so that his own comfort is no longer coincident with national thrift; he lights his fire with matches, he buys a new tin kettle every year instead of a solid copper one that holds a life time, he pays a rack rent for a jerry-built house that will last his slender tenure, he clothes his wife in a dress of fashionable shoddy, and he brings up his little brood of consumers under conditions of such uniform ugliness that they shall neither desire nor seek for Beauty when they enter into their generation. Meantime the producer says, "Where is this going to end ? Am I the better for your extravagance, you thriftless loon ? Whether you drink champagne, or sodden beer, is it improving me? " Let us take a walk from Mile End to Bond Street. What in the world have I been doing ? What is the good of all this truck ? Come, let us have a sorting out. In future it is *I* who shall determine what it pleases me to make, and you may conform your tastes to my production. That is to say, stripped of metaphor, those who are re-constructing the workshop will not consider their task accomplished till every article is produced under pleasurable conditions, and inasmuch as the underlying optimism in us prompts us, other things being equal, to make a good article, rather than a bad one, the consumer's standard of choice will be raised by the rise of the producer's standard of comfort.

24

The circle of my propositions on the need for the cultiva- Social
tion of the sense of Beauty, is therefore rounded off by the last, problems
namely, that the social problems of the present day have claims to
prior claim to the artistic; "the best decoration for an artistic
empty house" being, as has been wisely said, "a flitch of
bacon." In truth, both the senior partner of Messrs. Sky
Sign & Co., and Mr. Thomas Trudge the workman, though
they have but little in common, are at one in this matter
absolutely, and it was interesting to note how they each ·
took the quotation from Ruskin. Mr. Pushington said
solemnly, "Yes, indeed, that's true; very true!" Mr. Trudge
nodded assent and laughed, happy-go-lucky. I don't know
if the former thought, as he spoke, of the Leighton he had
just purchased for his drawing-room, but I know the latter
regarded his oleographs as potential bacon, for he jerked
his pipe at them while speaking. Only Mr. Trudge and Mr.
Pushington differ fundamentally as to how the social problems are to be worked out, and of the two, I think Mr.
Trudge's policy, and I will tell you more of both in due
place, appears more constructional—it is certainly more
definite. He, at least, is sure, Mr. Pushington is not sure
at all, except that things are wrong, that things are giving
way, that what he would like to keep as a social order,
he can only keep by virtue of his own personal prestige
and strength of character; and that is why he heads the
Liberals in S.W. Kensington.

Indeed, to the majority of us, there is no room for the
cultivation of the sense of Beauty. We need more leisure
to do it—we want more holidays. My friend, Mr. Thomas
Trudge, once furnished me with an interesting little personal
experience of his, which illustrates my meaning. I asked
him how he spent his holidays when he got them. I do not
mean his occasional Bank Holidays, but the *long* holidays—
his week in the Summer. Well, he spent it with the wife
and kids at Margate; but he had to read the *Chronicle* all
the morning and the *Star* all the evening, because he was
so bored, and if it hadn't been for the little ones, he'd as
lief have stayed at home, because not only did it cost him so
much out of pocket, but he forfeited the two pounds
ten which he would have drawn on his week's job. Reading
the labour movement at Margate when you are living in it
all the year round, is much like the holiday the 'busman
takes when, after his monthly fifteen hours a day, he has a
day off, and spends it driving round with a pal on another
'bus. One would seem almost to be speaking in irony in
saying that it is to this man that we have to entrust the
future of the sense of Beauty.

The middle-class Englishman and his care for Beauty is to me, well typified, and the better because unconsciously, by Mark Twain's "Yankee at the Court of King Arthur." This brute of an American, with whom one is supposed to sympathise, describes the wonders of the Camelot he is about to destroy; the palace with its carvings, its metal work, its woven hangings, and then says, "But there was one thing I missed—there was no Art. Now if there's one thing I like, it's a little Art, but there wasn't even an oleograph." That is the ordinary British conception of Art, something outside life, something to be bought, if you can afford it ; after gratifying your other vulgar tastes, something to hang upon a wall, and something, above all, something that will pay.

The term "to pay," when closely examined, implies immediate and superficial results; it implies what can be got in the shape of comforts, pleasures' desires, for a definite expenditure of capital; and these comforts, pleasures, desires, are strictly commensurate with the character and mental development of the individual. He, as a rule, is a vulgar or half-taught person, and holds, what has been fancifully termed, "low" or "unclean" ideals; that is to say, he prefers an Adelphi melo-drama to Shakespeare, piousness to Albert Chevalier, and a City gorge to a minuet. You will observe, however, that he reserves a qualifying phrase likewise redolent of metaphor, and borrowed with subtle British instinct from the Turf, and he says, it does pay "in the long run ;" this qualification is his salvation. To culti- vate the sense of Beauty does pay in the long run; it is worth our while as a nation to do it. - Beauty, I. repeat, is meant for the enjoyment of man, but its understanding comes before its enjoyment. To understand, we must re-construct the workshop and re-model the citizen con- currently, and, in spite of the unwholesome precepts of St. Paul, and their natural outcome in 17th century puritanism, 18th century torpor, and 19th century godliness and commerce, I venture to think Christ knew what He was about when he presided at the Marriage of Cana, and turned the water into wine.

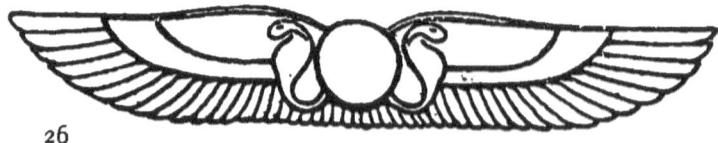

CHAPTER 3.—HOW CAN WE "RUN" ART AT OUR POLYTECHNICS?

A PAPER READ AT
THE BIRMINGHAM
ART CONGRESS, 1891.

When I forwarded the title of this chapter to the austere authorities of the Birmingham Art Congress, they revised the word "run" into the word "foster." My explanation was that I wrote "run," because I meant the verb transitive; theirs that they wrote "foster" as a more classic reading of "run." We both had our intentions, doubtless, and I hope to show what were mine in firmly adhering to the more expressive vernacular.

Suppose I were to begin by stating frankly that we cannot "run" art at our polytechnics, and that the one thing we ought not to do is to "foster" it; and I will say at once that that is my candid opinion, but I will qualify it with another, not by any means a quibble, and that is that we might, under certain conditions, let it "run"—verb intransitive. It is in the nature of the Englishman to "run" things; as the man of a type, he would be the strong man organising; but when he comes athwart something that will not be organised, he gets into trouble—and such a thing is Art.

Here is the sketch of what would, to me, seem the most rational form for polytechnic development. The industry of the district is our first consideration, and this is determined by the manufactory or great business which supplies it. From this springs the need for affiliating the school to the factory, and this school should be polytechnic or technical school, in other words *the teaching function and the workshop function should be combined.* Given the need for a teaching in artistic principles in any industry, it is the head designer of the factory who should be the leading teacher in the school, and his pupils should have the

27

entrance into the factory where the corporate and educational work of the school should develop into a similar work for life and bread. As for the system of the school, it should not be conducted by means of a series of random classes but by what one might call application lessons : design applied directly to material. Many social and economic forces have to to be taken into account before such a system is attainable. It would not be impossible, however, to work at one or another of these points in any polytechnic according as the industry admitted of it, leaving the rest to be done by Tendency,—the 19th century's unknown god. We have, however, two difficulties before us, the one legislative, the other industrial, both affecting immediately not only the development of the polytechnics, but that of the artistic growth within them ; the one is what one might term the pachydermatous flatulence of the South Kensington system, the other a much greater difficulty, the industrial relations of English manufacture.

The Mummy   Our policy at present, when we find a man who has in him the making of a polytechnic, or the power of a teacher of applied art, is to tie his right arm to his left leg with tape, and bid him see what he can make of it. He does his best, and under the circumstances it is often wonderful what he does make of it. He is burdened with the incubus of " Will it pay ? " and he has to get his dispensation for Art creativeness from the old mummy of the central department. 'Tis a wonderful creature, this mummy : it sits there with no head, or what head of it there is, centralised in the clouds ; it sits with legs crossed, hands crossed and forefingers pointed passively ; elbows resting on its chair, and around it the withes of red tape, its top hat on the ground beside. You cry to it, but how can it hear you ? You ask of it utterance, and oracularly it answers, " I am that I am." Even so, wonderful ! But still the polytechnics are springing up around it.

Industrial difficulties   As regards the other, the industrial difficulty, we say, marry the polytechnics to the industries ; and we are bidden to take counsel from our German neighbours in matters of industrial education, see their schools and the affiliation between these and their factories. True, but our difficulty in England is different from theirs. Having a more developed commercialism, we have likewise a more developed system of industrial organisation and divided labour. There is our *impasse*. The problem of industrial education is to be firmly

28

gripped, but by whom, by the masters or by the men? The obvious answer is—by both. But will they combine? Give the designer and the workman each his fair place and prominence, is asked on the one hand, and on the other it is answered, the system will not admit of it, nor can I afford to do it. Both question and answer are sound. *The points of view of manufacturer, designer, and workman*

I will put those questions and replies in a more direct and human form. Here are the personalities as I have myself had thé honour of knowing them. I have heard from their own lips their several positions, and, I may add, unbeknown to each other.

There is, first of all, my friend Mr. Archibald Pushington, the head partner of the well-known firm, Messrs. Sky Sign and Co. I have had the frequent honour of dining at his house in Kensington, where I have met with much artistic and intellectual society. His sons and daughters are artistic and intellectual, and we have invariably at his dinner table discussed Tendency. He is the kindest of men, subscribes largely to an experiment in technical education in which I am interested, and always takes my advice on artistic matters; we are great friends. There is then Mr. John Pennyworth. I met him by chance at South Kensington one Saturday afternoon as we were sketching from the same Sicilian diaper in the Silk Room. We struck up an acquaintance, and he invited me finally to his villa at Tottenham, where we had high tea under the discreet auspices of Mrs. Pennyworth, who divided her attention between the partially trained domestic and the conversation at table; a little too high for her, for it was a conversation on Tendency. There is then Mr. Thomas Trudge, the work-man. He is a strong Trade-unionist, and takes the chair at benefit societies. It was leéturing at a workman's club once on Ruskin that I happened to make his acquaintance. He asked me questions, and we got into communication. I promised to lend him " Time and Tide," and, being one day in the neighbourhood of Burdett Road, Mile End, thought I would take him the book myself. It happened to be washing day when I called, and the family were disconcerted at my inopportune visit. Matters had to be made good somehow, and so I was invited to supper and a pipe on the Sunday. While Mrs. Trudge was putting the small children to bed we talked Tendency.

Now the points of view of these three friends of mine, setting aside the opinions on Tendency which each held,

Mr. Push- were somewhat as follows :—Mr. Pushington was kindly
ington's pleased with the interest that I showed in the big house;
point of especially in its relation to the foreign market. My ideas,
view he thought, were a bit unpractical, but none the less
suggestive, and he intended to try and work some of them
out. As regards the problem of design applied to manufacture, and the position of the designer, of course, what I said
was perfctly true, the designer ought to be brought forward
and his name be known ; but then the fact of competiton
had to be faced—it was not so serious, perhaps,—but if
Messrs. Driver and Shootforth, of Manchester, for instance,
his principal competitors in the Belgian market, saw an
open list of his best men, they would overbid at once, and
how could he prevent their going ? For his part, he would
be only too glad to raise their salaries, though it *was* the
case that they were earning from £50 to £500 a year—he
was proud to say, as handsome an average wage as was
given by any firm for draughtsmanship—but the matter
must be fairly worked out with the understanding of other
large firms. Then, too, there were the traditions of Sky
Sign and Co. Surely they had to be considered ? It was
no mean work that his uncle and his grandfather had
accomplished before him ; and, finally, there was the big
question of the responsibility of capital, which, of course,
nobody can fully understand unless he is really in the within.
Did he know a Mr. Pennyworth ? Oh, yes, a most able
draughtsman in the H department—a very clever fellow,
whom the firm were much indebted to, and could not afford
to lose. Curious that I should be acquainted with him—
very glad to hear me speak so well of his little place at
Tottenham—thought it was Tooting—often wanted to send
Pennyworth to Italy for three months—only too glad to pay
his expenses—fellow wouldn't accept—home ties or something—too conservative—curious. Did he know any of the
men in the factories personally ? No, how could he ? You
see there are so many of them, and then there was always
the Trade-union difficulty to be faced. He was glad to say
that in his place there was a perfect understanding between
himself and the men, and if he had only his own people to
deal with, the thing would be easy enough, but then there
were those agitators, who led the men astray, and put
foolish notions in their heads, and, after all, what could be
more destructive both to the interests of labour and capital
than a strike ?—it was the poor fellows themselves who

suffered most. How did the Art question affect the
workman? Not at all, he should say. The subdivision of
labour, the use of machinery, and the growth of civilisation
necessitated a firmly organised arrangement of industry.
The workman nowadays was only what you might call a
"*productive*" particle. The designer, on the other hand,
was a man who had to master the theory of his subject, and
he was the "*conceptive*" particle; and then, finally, there
came the strong, exploiting, organising, developing force of
capital. He himself was, of course, only a small link in the
whole revolving chain—a particle too, if you like, the
"*impelling*" particle which gave life and activity to the
other two. That was Mr. Pushington's position.

Now the position of Mr. Pennyworth, the designer, was Mr.
different and yet analogous. It grudgingly accepted the Penny-
"particle theory," and strove to assert a handicapped point of
individualism. Had he anything to complain of? Nothing view
in the world; Mr. Pushington was the kindest of men, and
the junior partners, all of them, were zealous in the observa-
tion of duty, honour, and fairness to all their employés.
That made it all the more difficult to grumble, all the more
immoral to grumble, all the more unmannerly to grumble.
He had a good salary, a comfortable home, nice books.
Yes,—he had read Ruskin, and believed in him; but, then,
what was he, a single Pennyworth, to do in the world, with
a number of small Pennyworths dependent upon him? He
admitted the unreasonableness of his position; he knew it
was wrong that his designs, the boiling down of his brains,
should be vaunted at exhibitions as Messrs. Sky Sign and
Co.'s latest achievements; but what could he do? He was
their servant nursed by them into comfort. Without them
what had he to fall back upon? A South Kensington
certificate, framed, in Tommy's bedroom! They had always
acted handsomely to him, and then there was such a thing
as loyalty in the world, and it was a great thing, a really
great thing, to see the "Boss" give an order, and see how
all obeyed it. Did he know any of the workmen? Well,
yes and no. You see the wife had to be considered, not that
he minded—his people had been working people themselves,
and he had bettered himself, as was only right that every
man should who could. But he sympathised with their
position; he was a Radical himself, a bit of a Socialist, too.
But then, what did the workman know about Art? Come
now! He could tell from the experience of many years

how impossible it was to leave anything to the men to carry out. He had to issue his instructions from the H department with infinite accuracy in every detail, figured and drawn on paper. True, the old Gothic and Italian people did not work like that; but then we were in the nineteenth century and not in the Middle Ages. That was a fact, and the thing was just this—Art, it could only be in the actual design nowadays, for the subdivision of labour was such that where there were twenty different hands employed in the making of a particular piece of work there was only one designer. Could it all be altered? He hoped so; yes, verily it *was* wrong as it was! And so over the warm grog which we drank together, the soul of Pennyworth expanded and rebelled.

Mr. Trudge's point of view

The position of Mr. Thomas Trudge, 193, Burdett Road, Mile End, E., was much more extreme. It was less cultured, it was certainly more limited. First of all, he did not care much for matters as I stated them to him. That was as much as to say, I must either converse in his conversation, or not converse at all. He was dogmatic, he was intolerant, he was ignorant—I mean ignorant of conversational delicacy. The problem of industry—I began with industry, not with Art. How was it to be solved? Sure he could not say. Some few things might be abolished, perhaps, with advantage. The great question was the labour question—wages—how to raise the standard—how to get the men to combine. You see the ordinary workman was very near the margin of subsistence. What he thought of first was how to get his week's money—that was just a fact— straight! As for Mr. Pushington—he had only seen him once, once in his life—rather a good sort of man—a fine, square head. But, bless you, what had Mr. Pushington to do with things? The business was the business, and as good as any other house he should say; but it was the machine that he was fighting with, and when the union struck for a rise, they struck on principle and not on Pushington. That large profits were made he had heard, because his cousin's sister was lady's-maid at some duke's, who had once bought a thing that had been made by his bench-mate, and we knew what he got for that job! But no doubt that was all right. Working expenses had to be paid, &c., &c.; it was not *that* he was fighting for. Could the workmen work out things for themselves? Yes, if you could get them to forego the temptations of small mastership. Co-operative Societies?—

32

perhaps ; questionable! They usually failed for want of a common policeman? Art? What did I mean? He liked pictures when he saw them. He had seen some pictures by Holman Hunt once that he thought grand,—so did the missus. He did not know that I meant Art when I referred to the designs of the H. department. That was a new light to him. As for himself, you could hardly expect much in the drawing line from a man who worked eight or nine hours a day at his bench, and had been doing so since the age of fourteen. Yes, he was glad to see his boy Jack was fond of drawing, but he did not know what it was going to lead to. These polytechnics? H'm! well, all *that*, sir, had to be taken with a grain of salt! That was what Mr. Thomas Trudge thought of it ; and so I compared notes of the positions of my three friends.

Now, how does all this affect our polytechnics and the Art teaching in its relation to industry, which we want to "stimulate," not "foster," within them? Simply thus, that it is by these three men that the polytechnics have to be made. Mr. Pushington is invited to initiate and give the funds, Mr. Pennyworth is invited to teach, and Mr. Trudge is invited to come and be taught.

But are we not met by a difficulty? Mr. Pushington is hampered by the perfectness of his own organisation ; the men who are to be taught decline the offer, and the social and economic conditions make genuine teaching—not teaching for a narrow groove—a questionable possibility. Mr. Pennyworth is ignorant of the tool, and Trudge is ignorant of the design, and not desirous of knowing anything about it. Labour is divided between the theory and the reality, the conception is divorced from the fulfilment.

Now I do not propose in this chapter to go deeply into the question of workshop re-construction. I would not even suggest the immediate conversion of Mr. Pushington into an industrial partnership, and so make his men part of him, even supposing productive co-operation a possibility ; so for the present we may leave his great organisation to work out its own destinies through the stages of limited liability, and the balance of strikes and compromises. We believe in the unknown god—Tendency. But we can do something for Mr. Pennyworth and the H department, and we might insinuate something for the service of Mr. Trudge and his union, always remembering that Mr. Trudge is the conservative force, and Mr. Pushington the liberal and advanced thinker. We will see

33

what might be done, then, in this more limited sphere, but we will see, first, what actually *is* done.

How polytechnics are formed

This is what *is* done. The polytechnic fever sweeps over Kensington. Mr. Pushington offers £20,000; the secretaries of the associations for the promotion of technical and commercial and other education are secured; the Worshipful Company of Corkscrew Drivers assist with a handsome endowment, and the *Times* draws on its solemn cothurnus, and strides down before a delighted public with a dithyrambic leader. Then more money comes in, and then come in the Charity Commissioners, and close with a complementary £40,000; the buildings are built by an eminent architect, and the place is opened by the Princess— I forget which. Everything booms along magnificently. But what is actually done inside? Why, classes are started— classes, of course—classes! They are educational things these classes, and so there they go, classes in carpentry, classes in metal work, classes in leather, classes in cabinet-making, classes in modelling, classes in boot-blacking, classes in bicycles, classes in letter-sorting, classes in anything reasonable or unreasonable, with a view to the application of Art to Industry.

This, I venture to think, is a mistake. It is not classes that we want; it is Art as a whole that we have to consider— the "classee" as an individual, with the possibility of an idea in him. This pitter-patter of hammers, this decking of boys in the fringes and tassels of trades (done by a pupil under fourteen, as the card says on the exhibit); this pinching of iron with the fingers; this carving of wood, characteristically called "chip;" this copying of lithographic reproductions, cousins many times removed of the Greek Acanthus, translated from its classic purity by Mr. Poynter; and the many other wickednesses of all this greatness; the want of discipline and the want of unity, and the want of *esprit de corps*, every man doing his own little bit of dilettantism for his own little self, coming there for his own culture and his own pleasure, no feeling of the greatness of combination that there might be in so great a whole. It is because we would do so much that we do so little. Why so fine and large? 'Tis not necessary for them all to be 80,000 pounders; they would be much easier to work small, they would be healthier, more human, more genuine. Let us have smaller, less pretentious polytechnics, and we should be able to do much more work within them.

34

Now I have a suggestion to make to Mr. Pushington. Suppose he were to keep his £20,000. Suppose he were to spend the interest of it upon the educational development, is artistic matters of the employées of Sky Sign and Co. Suppose he were to build a small hall, with benches, books, and appliances, useful and illustrative of the trade of Sky Sign and Co. Suppose he were then to say to Mr. Pennyworth, now complete your knowledge by a more careful application to the tools and concrete facts of design ; and to Mr. Trudge, now come and improve not your technical skill, but master some of the theory of your trade, and learn how the whole hangs together. In addition, suppose he taught in his school the small Pennyworths and the small Trudges the use of the tool and the use of the pencil alike, and got them in their boyhood to feel this relation of Art to industry, got them to see the charm of a well-lit, well-hung hall of Art and Industry, got them to feel their own little relation to Sky Sign and Co. ; perhaps even insuring them a footing through their pupilage in the school into the historic house itself. That, it seems to me, would be a veritable polytechnic, and a genuine application of Art to Industry.

And there would be no need to ask aid of the effete mummy in a case like this. The historic house could do all itself. In part, co-operatively, by endowment from the firm, and by fees from the pupils. Then carry the principle further. Suppose several historic houses combined and started a school in the district, and in the midst of some local industry ; that, I venture to think, would be a still nobler development.

I once heard of a case of this nature. A school of—well, what shall I say ?—I must not attach verbiage to facts—let me call it a school for the teaching apprentices how to make—I choose something remote—how to make golden shuttles, an article of luxury much required by the surrounding community ; a demand had arisen for the application of Art to the Industry of the golden shuttle, and so the school was founded. Everything was complete. There was a large room, with lathes and benches and tools of all descriptions and assortments, all made in Birmingham by the best makers. There were designs of golden shuttles from the old masters, every historical period illustrated, plaster casts and reproductions and advice to students, and everything that mortal could desire who wanted to design, create, and finally perfe&t for purpose of love or sale the required commodity—the golden shuttle. But there was one flaw in the whole system, and it was this: by some curious law the master designer, himself in his youth a distinguished golden shuttle maker, was not allowed to work in the school with his own hands—not allowed to produce. That was a noble English anomaly. Conceive the *premier maçon* in the Gothic cathedral with his workmen around him and not allowed to touch the chisel; conceive the master painter in his studio with his pupils about him and not allowed touch the brush! Design, is twofold, spirit and flesh, the idea and the manipulation, the sense of the form, the human, the colour, or whatever it is that impels; and the sense of the tangible, the plastic, the material, or whatever it is that receives. You can as little sever the one from the other as paint a pi&ture with good intentions or carve a capital with sound advice.

How Polytech- nics might be formed But I return to the polytechnic. We have still to consider what might be done. Suppose the mischief achieved, suppose the boom a success, and the big building run up, all yellow brick backing, iron girder and renaissance façade—vast and improper. What are we to do inside it? Consult the mummy! is the first thing everybody says. But can't we do without the mummy for once if the endowment be big enough? If the drudgery for grants has to be gone through to a certain degree, well then we must needs draw chins, and stipple the plaster cast of Michael Angelo's Moses' nose up to the requisite pitch, only do not let us be persuaded that it is applying Art to Industry or even industry to Art. What then, what ought we to do? For my part, I think that the first thing we have to do is to accept the principle of mastership. The mastership, not of a department, but of an individual. First, we must have our good master, and we must pay him well. Then we might have him controlled, or guided possibly on occasion, by a committee of experts; men who understand the study of decorative Art in the more general sense, each in their own line, archite&ts, or designers, or painters; with these experts we should put some business men, who have a pra&tical knowledge of the market, and of the openings in the Industry in qustion. But it is your master, who is the important man, he who will give his life to it, the man on whom your school's future depends, and the most important things about him are his own creative capacity, and his relation to his pupils. A man is

36

no good as a master for having passed standards only, that is a paper qualification; he is no good as a master for having technical power only, that is a metallic or a wooden qualification; or, at least, one limited to the stuff which he works,—but the greatness of a good master is that he himself produces, and that he also works in men as much as in metals, wood, and paper,—he must have something magnetic about him. Hence the pupils must have their say in the choice of the master. It is the pupil who is the master's best judge. Therefore, the students at our poly-technics should, as far as possible, elect their own master. It is this that was done in the Middle Ages at the universities, when the boy scholars came to hear a good teacher; it is this which gives vitality to the outside ateliers of modern Paris, and the same end should be attained, though it can only be so done by slow degrees, at our polytechnics.

How to make for it? I answer by letting the students, pupils, workmen, be as independent and self-governing as possible; by inviting representations from the Unions and trade bodies and clubs of the district in which your polytechnic is to be. This seems to me the only way to work the matter out, for if we start with too lordly a benevolence from above, the men we seek will remain for us unfound. If the prestige of the master is the first principle to be observed within the polytechnic, the second must be the fellowship of the students, and so the school will grow to a corporate whole, in which the students feel a life, and for which they feel a reverence. "In the reverence of my master Andrea, and of his master Taddeo, and of his master Giotto;" that is how the old Italian began his treatise on painting; it is that spirit which we want to see reborn amoug us. And it is Art, and especially handicraft, loyally and traditionally developed, that can bring it to birth.

Polytechnics, in so far as they deal with Art, should be genuine schools of handicraft—we shall be better for keeping to the honest Saxon word—and the Art that we want to develop in those schools should be of a three-fold nature. It should be personal, it should in time be traditional, and it should, above all, be corporate. The student, the workman, the youth, is attracted to the school individually; but he is held corporately, he should carry the traditions of his school with him to the end of his life, and bequeath them as a sacred memory to his children.

Indeed, much could be made of these polytechnics if they were absorbed into the local Industry, and, where Art is needed, all could be centred round the Art impetus wisely developed within them. But nothing can be done except it be done through the rank and file. Once bring the question of Art home to the life of the man you want to win, and it will be a question no longer; and this, if we are really in earnest about the application of Art to Industry, is what we must do. Personally I believe there is Art in the Englishman's nature; but it cannot be "run" for him, it cannot be advertised out of him, the *Times* cannot do it, nor the Charity Commissioner, nor the millionaire. It can only be won from him little by little, coaxed from him. Give him his chances, and he will find it himself.

One final, inevitable reflection is forced upon us therefore, and, that is, we cannot as yet hope for any genuine Art teaching at the polytechnics. Art, the higher production be it remembered, is the final outcome of the reconstructed workshop. As at present constituted the polytechnics are and remain outside the workshop, and until they are merged into, and become part of the workshop, this will continue. It is not difficult to conceive of the possibility of the Industry of the future, perhaps of the near future, being conducted on a more co-operative, a less individualistic basis, and by combination among the different producers. In this case the further possibility suggests itself that the different polytechnics which we are now establishing will find their right place, and be utilised by the newer system for the higher workshop training. Of these possible industrial developments, as they bear upon Art and Craft I shall have more to say in a future chapter; for the present, however, the conclusion that is forced upon us is that the polytechnics are excellent institutions, that they may fulfil many useful functions, and may do much towards the forming of the future citizens, but that they are outside the direct educational and creative issues of life and of the workshop, and that Art, that is to say, the higher production, has no place within them.

CHAPTER 4.—DECORA-
TIVE ART FROM A WORK-
SHOP POINT OF VIEW.

A PAPER READ TO THE
EDINBURGH ART CON-
GRESS, 1889.

The key to the study of most things nowadays is the social question; hence, if we want to study the Art question in any other than its immediate bearing on ourselves, we must approach it from the same point of view. Every artist or craftsman works out, consciously or not, some portion of what might be termed the social aspect of the Art problem, in painting, in architecture, in handicraft alike. Is his line portraiture, the spirit forces in the portraits of Watts will appeal to him. Does he affect Burne-Jones, he will see the nineteenth-century hero in the head of Perseus: is it church architecture he is dealing with, there will come home to him the sense of two conflicting forces, living vulgarity and dying antiquarianism. If he be bitten with Paris, there are the the confessions of George More for a stumbling-block. As for Naturalism it will bring with it its honest acceptance of modern ugliness. In Impressionism the great moments of our civilisation may be flashed upon him. While the lower forms of Art will reveal a still closer bearing on social questions; beauty-in-use will be brought before him, cheap-and-nasty will be his bugbear; and trans-cending all questions of style or school, the great question of the life of leisure will come upon him with silent insistence. How much leisure have I, how has it come to me, what justifiability is there for it in my case; to what purpose of communal service am I placing it?

The object of this chapter, starting with the recognition of the social bearings of Art, is to suggest the application to the Art problem, and to the question of Art development, the ideals and practicalities of an ordinary nineteenth-century workshop, in the belief that a purer and healthier condition both of industrial activity, and artistic sensitiveness can only be attained by a combination of the two.

To start with the aphorism that Art must be carried on in the workshop and not in the studio, in the face of the fact that all the great Art work of the present day has been carried on in the studio and not the workshop, appears at first sight a paradox: but it is easy of explanation. In the first place, we are dealing with Art as a whole, and not with picture-painting; in the second place, we are dealing with

39

decorative Art, in which the painting of a picture is a matter of minor importance : this accepted, the aphorism will not be difficult of establishment.

I do not wish it to be taken as in any sense for or against either, but I should draw the distinction between the workshop and the studio somewhat in the following manner.

Work-shop and studio

The studio is a happily situated nest, somewhere in the region of villas and top hats; it is built of red bricks, even if cheaply. It is fitted with all the apparatus necessary for the lighting, lifting, and wheeling to and from exhibitions of the large masterpiece; and it is ornamented with all the conventional gusto of the prevalent Queen in Anne-ity. Within there are scraps of damask silk, bartered from Roman curiosity shops, divers " subjects " under way, various Madonnas of the future, suggestions of decorative work sprayed upon the odd moments of panels. There is a cast from Pheidias, a photogravure of Millet, a skeleton and a lay figure. In the corner a pair of embroided slippers, and on the mantel-piece pipes and tobacco. The inmate for whom these things have their being, works hard, appreciates the silence and solitude of his surroundings, and is comfortably conscious of his Bohemianism. In the afternoon there are lady visitors, and the servant brings in five o'clock tea.

The workshop is almost as light as the studio, though less pleasantly situated, and near the racket of some big thoroughfare. But what matters noise ? if there be noise without, there is noise within; hammering and sawing, and what not. Nor are the internal surroundings as pleasant to look on. Blue whitewash takes the place of damask fragments, and moveable gas jets of patent reflectors. The place is in a condition in which no house-wife would enter it and the glue pot is simmering on the stove pipe. As to the fittings, there are benches, and racks for tools, also possibly a small furnace, and a good deal of grime. To hang up prints there would be inadvisable, though a photolithographic advertisement assists in telling the days of the week, and offers an appropriate quotation for the better committing them to memory. As to the rest the furniture consists of rows of pegs, on which hang hats, coats, and aprons; here and there a teapot with a broken spout, and an occasional coloured kerchief containing two plates, bound face-wise. The inmates of the workshop pursue their avocation with the regularity of clock-work ;—a light in their faces, perhaps, of an armed resistance to something—and the dinner hour at twelve o'clock is enlivened with the perusal and discussion of racy paragraphs from a halfpenny radical print.

These, to my mind, are the two pictures; but I hold that in the higher sense the proper place of decorative Art is the latter; and I repeat the aphorism that Art must be carried on in the workshop, not in the studio.

In the first place, the right understanding of forms of orna- ment,—elements of design, is only possible in their direct bearing on forms of material,—elements of construction. You need your basis of matter wherein to engender the spirit. You must understand the stone, the wood, the pigments, the clay, what each can do, what its limitations are; and this means an understanding, if, merely for the sake of conceiving our own incapacity to use them, of the tools that are the guardians of these limitations. " Rivington's," that famous tome on building construction, whose pyramidal ascent of facts has to be scaled before youthful architects pass Royal Institute examinations, would lose half its value if it were not for the isolation of the architect's studio, euphemistically termed his office; but a half-hour in the workshop would save days of fruitless drudgery over its pages. I received the other day, from the head-master of a provincial board-school, a letter saying that his board desired him to teach the use of tools; could I assist him, what text-books was he to read up, and could a list of the tools be provided? I recommended, not " Rivingtons " but a carpenter to take the head-master's place.

The ways are innumerable in which the workshop alone can instruct in the limitations of material, and the functions of the tool; every hour in the workshop reveals something, whether it be so small a matter as the pressure of the sable which produced the favourite form of the Gothic painted leaf, or so great a matter as the thrust of the arch which produced that identical ogeeval curve in architectural construction. The study of these limitations is complex enough for us, without our losing the accumulated benefit of workshop experience and practicalities. We may go home to our studios and copy realistically if we will; but given the knack, it always remains easier to copy realistically than to master the limitations of material.

A historical study of Art forms is, perhaps, one of the most fascinating things possible, and would be calculated to throw much light on decorative art from the workshop point of view. If we were to tell an every-day artist that his shoddy stucco frame is, in the eyes of the Creator, more of a work of art than his own landscape painting which it contains, the remark would savour of blasphemy: or if we were to point out to him that the same painting was actually

The limitations of material in either

D

41

a development of the frame itself, and that the genesis of the picture in the frame could be traced to the days when Margaritone illuminated the frameworks and crucifixes of Umbrian Altars with toilsome conventionalisations of the Christ, it would appear to him a mere antiquarian vagary, but, none the less, both statements might safely be asserted.

Thus much for the artistic principles contained in the ideas of studio and workshop respectively; and if the recording angel has even not yet thrown the chased goblet into the heavier scale of the latter, we have still all the human and vital elements, in the being of each, to take into account.

We might call the studio, in its nature, subjective; it fosters that refined sensuality of nineteenth century art, self-introspection, whereas the workshop has in it the elements of the human and objective. In the coming together of men, in the magnetic affinities that spring up between them, are the forces that engender Art creativeness, just as in academical life they give rise best to speculation and literary creativeness. Ideas may be conceived in solitude, but they are brought to birth by co-operation. Men take creative force from each other. Those psychical moments of which we now hear so frequently, imply men, in the union of number, in their combined readiness to accept the new idea. The ancients would have stated the case between the work-shop and the studio in the terms of Pantheism. Narcissus had a studio by the brookside, and he perished in the contemplation of his own loveliness; Vulcan had a workshop under Etna, and all men and gods marvelled at it, for it was grand and awful by virtue of the united and rhythmical ringing of its hammers.

When we set to work, however, to produce decorative Art in the workshop, there is forced upon us the problem of the subdivision of labour: how unsatisfactory and uneconomical any present system is, and how necessary a re-arrangement. But the question is, on what basis? The exigencies of the market determine the supply of the decorative commodity; certain goods are wanted, and have to be provided rapidly and largely; alter these exigencies, and you alter the conditions. As soon as people begin to feel the true connection between construction and design, the designer will at once be brought nearer the workshop. Architects will no longer build houses with half timber masks, nor designers paint landscapes on coal-scuttles. A newer division of labour will set in, by which the designer will work less on paper, and the workman less without it.

Bearing in mind that the great problem of the modern *The prob-* *lem of* workshop is organisation, there seems a curious fitness in *workshop* the application of its ways and methods to the question of *organi-* decorative Art, for decorative Art, from the very fact of its *sation* being so impersonal, admits of organisation. That ceaseless fund of willing labour, with which mankind is endowed, finds scope in it. The labour by which historical schools grow up, labour unoriginal, imitative, conscientious, diligent and humble; the labour which produced the intricacies of the monastic manuscript and the thousand crockets on the Gothic cathedral. For decorative Art on any large scale implies repetition, implies method, and the constant dwelling on and development of some one idea. It is as the variation on a theme in a symphony; for one man to do it is an impossibility; you need a hundred, with different instruments, before you can give your decorative theme its full value in variety.

And further, your organisation, just like your decoration, must have a soul in it. The thousand men who carve the crockets must have the sense of concerted action, even as the thousand crockets must artistically express unity; and so our next question is how this can be got, what is to be our substitute for the monastic ideal, or the creative enthusiasm of the guilds? There, again, the modern work-shop can come to our aid. Apply the militant spirit of trade unionism which more or less pervades the workshop —apply the growing instinct for co-operative action, whether for the purposes of attack, of distribution, or of pro-duction—and we may have a like spirit to that by which Athens of Pericles was perfected, or the England of William of Wykeham made beautiful.

The basis of the new subdivision of labour must, therefore, *Re-con-* *struction* be a sound one socially. In the Greek and Mediæval times, *towards a* labour was divided in a manner which we neither can nor need *new basis* seek to copy; we have merely to study results, and emulate with means and methods of our own. This end before us, and with the workshop as our basis of action, we have, as I conceive it, to reorganise the sub-division of labour from an anti-class point of view. We have first to recognize the dignity of all labour—dignity in service; we have secondly to recognise the equality of all labour—equality in service, but differing according to merit and capacity. We have, even as a wise collector does, to give equal rights to the Sèvres vase, and the chap book of hawkers' cries. True, they appealed to different publics in their day, but in the cupboard—each a work of decorative Art—they stand as man to man.

At present the class disunions are acute in proportion to their nearness; the workman despises the clerk, the clerk the workman; the wage of each is to all intents and purposes fixed and the same; the labour of one is as valuable to the community as the labour of the other; it is the artificial class barrier that does the mischief. A regards B as a snob or a renegade, B looks on A as an inferior being. None the less, however, the workshop is ready for reorganisation, only another force has to be introduced, and that is commuity of action. Community of action is already partially accomplished in our great armies of Industry and distributive agencies; the co-operative principle has only to be more fully applied. In decorative Art, where men are working for a creative purpose, and where their labour is in itself educational, this community of action can be more keenly felt, for it is a union, not only of pockets, but of hands and hearts. And its highest outcome will be style— style in workmanship, style in design, in decoration, in architecture, and ultimately, national style. Put your decorative Art into the workshop; united action is the steel workshop needs, and ingenuities are the flint, and from their contact the living spark will spring. We should regard decorative Art as a new heraldry; let our pupils, our workshops, and our communities, have badges, devices, trade-marks of their own. For there are great principles involved in the emblematic treatment of decorative Art. It implies an understanding of ornament in its repetition and development. It implies a soul within, which may have prompted its creation, and it implies community of action, because it can exist only where men are banded together for some common purpose. The signature of Turner on a picture is a personal matter, but the hand on the apprentice's column, the collar of S.S., the badges of the old guilds, the mark of P.R.B., imply an art principle within a co-operative force.

Solve the question of style in Art, and we at once find the solution of a still harder problem—that of our standard of criticism, the bane of every most enlightened and judicious hanging committee. We may, since the days of Sir Joshua, have produced schools of painting, but we have produced no schools of craft. Given the style, the schools' outcome, and at once we have the standard. At present the workman's only canon is technical excellence, and that of the average Englishman, so far as he can be said to have any at all, is a shallow realism. A landscape of Hunt's he judges good if it be like what he, in some beefy moment, has seen; a figure of Burne Jones, in purposeful convention,

44

is to him an affectation and an enigma. " I'm a plain man,
and I know what I want ":—admirable aphorism! but fitly
paraphrased as follows: " I'm an ignorant man, I know
what suits my ignorance, and I'm very proud of it." And
that was why Watts, in his solemn picture of Mammon, has
applied, to the modern god, the old Greek fable of Midas
with the ass's ears.

To come now to a further point, the direct application of The appli-
these ideas to Industry, we have to work by a decentralising cation of
the teach-
process. It is only in their application to each special ing to the
Industry in its own district, it is only by a frank acceptance district
of the ways and methods of the workshop as the men of the
workshop in those districts have in the course of generations
created them, and by a full recognition of the organising
solidarity of these ways and methods, that any healthy
growth or glory in decorative Art can be achieved. Is it
the Industry of silk or cotton which we want to benefit ? we
must teach our workmen and designers the evolution of
pattern from the East, the sweetness of the Sicilian damask,
the virtue of the Flemish diaper, and we must show them
how the social conditions of each Art epoch had reference
to the design in its manifold developments. Is it the
Industry of furniture and wood-work ? we must trace step by
step the historical sequence of church fittings, the Gothic
screen, the Jacobean pulpit, we must show how the Art of
architecture in England, or the Art of painting in Italy,
fashioned the Art of cabinet-making ; whether in the reredos
or the wedding chest, and we must trace the intricacies of
construction and design, from the solid carpentry of the
Norman into the veneer of Louis Seize. If our Industry be
iron, we have the relation of the wrought to the cast ; the
work of those nameless artists whose craft adorns the
fireplaces of English country houses, or the cunning
workmanship of the Canterbury screens and the Hampton
Court gates. Is the local industry silver ?—that most
degraded of all modern English crafts—we can trace the
history of its decline under the Georges, through the Art of
Holland into the splendour of the Spanish renaissance, and
back to its crowning glory in the Middle Ages—the
sacramental cup. If we are dealing with the Industry of
colour-making, it is our business to apply the craft of the
Van Eycks, of Cennino Cennini, to modern manufacture,
and not only to bring to bear scientific skill to purity of
making, but artistic sensitiveness to the development of
lights and tones of colour in their decorative significance.
But in each and every instance if it is the workman we want

45

to train, it is of the workman we must tell; each school, each epoch, the Industry produced in each country, must be treated in its relation to the social conditions of the men whose impress is left upon it. This, I hold, is the only way of ultimately applying English decorative ability to English industry, and it is this that I should call the application to decorative Art, as far as education goes, of the workshop of the nineteenth century.

As to the ways and means, they are ready to hand. Congresses and public meetings of artists and others are our ventilating machine, exhibitions like those of the Arts and Crafts are the agencies for bringing the public in touch with the workshop; then there is the instinct for co-operation growing up within it, and there is the movement for the establishment of polytechnics and other technical institutions, which should add the element of school and educational dignity; of these I shall have more to say in a later chapter. Whether they are being developed aright is another question, and one which I will not in this chapter take into consideration ; but, as the experience which has supplied its material and given birth to its confidence has been drawn from the growth and development of workshops, schools, the artistic creativeness and the general labour movement in one of the workmen's quarters of London, it may not be out of place, from time to time, to draw upon this experience by way of illustration. Indeed, I should hold it needless on my part to speak as a theorist on these points, or even to speak at all, were I not myself engaged in constructive work. The days of artistic speculation are gone by ; all that concerns us now is the method of applying those truths which most artists and thinkers concur in holding. The work which my colleagues and I are doing, in East London, strives, in a certain measure, to realise the healthier conditions of decorative Art and workmanship in general, to which this and other chapters seek to call attention.

Attitude of the workman To continue the question of the workman's interest, and the workman's education toward those healthier conditions, I hold you can do nothing unless you give him representation. You accuse the workman of a want of ideas and a want of interest, but he has one all-absorbing idea, and one over-mastering interest : and that is the problem of industry and its re-organisation. If you want him to grow interested in art matters, you must put them to him in his own terms. Offer him the art problem as a problem of workshop organisation, and he will solve it for you. Here, again, the

46

workshop steps in. You cannot work out the problem of technical education in the teeth of the opposition of the Trade Unions: regard it merely as a means for benefiting English Industry to the interest of the masters, and it will be ephemeral; regard it as a national matter, and it will live. And this holds good not only of our workshops, but of our exhibitions and of polytechnics and technical schools. It is a question of what we risk—is it to be a vulgar democracy or an exotic art? For my part, speaking as an artist, I should say trust in the Democracy, for the Art can only be worked out through its agency.

Exactly the same applies to polytechnics, whether in Polytech-representation or in education. Polytechnics and technical nics again schools can only develope by becoming, in the fullest sense, People's universities; by being brought to bear directly on the industries of the locality in which they are situated, and by having on their governing bodies the representation, loyally and frankly given, of the working men who, through their trade societies and clubs, are seeking to reconstruct English Industry within the workshop.

To take the case of any of the newly created Polytechnics, nothing, from a workman's point of view, can be more out of sympathy with the conditions of London labour and workshops than their complete absence of representation; nothing, from an artist's point of view, is more hopeless for the ultimate improvement of the Industries of the district in which they are situate, than their methods of Art education. You cannot win your workmen's sympathies unless you work through them; offer them endowments from above, and they will leave them to the middle class; give them representative power, and they are with you. And, as for education in Art, it must be of the best, or not at all. Art, in any direct bearing on Industry, can only be taught by men who can themselves create, whether in design or workmanship. Better than make of our schools and polytechnics South Kensington Cram Shops, let us give up the idea of Art teaching altogether, for the destinies of English handicraft and Industry will assuredly be worked out without them.

To sum up. The points I have insisted on are these : The Art problem must be worked out through the social problem. The home of decorative Art must be the workshop, not the studio. In working our decorative Art on a large scale we must reorganise the subdivision of labour, and we must reorganise it on an anti-class basis. We must apply to decorative Art the principles of the workshop, especially those

47

co-operative ideals growing up in our midst, and we shall find in the development of the workshop the solution of the problems of style and criticism in Art and Craft. Finally, we must have, in our exhibitions, schools, and polytechnics, complete representation from workmen in their societies. Thus alone can the workshop be reconstructed, and a noble national Art in the end be created. The great question of the consumption of its commodities—the question from the point of view of the public outside, which I touched upon in my second chapter, and leave for later consideration ; but the workshop from within may suggest ways and means for this also. The destinies of British Art, Craft, and Industry must eventually be decided by the British working classes ; even as they are at present slowly and surely solving our social and economic questions, and in the end it may yet be told how, from the obscene bulb of the plutocracy, sprang the tulip of the new civilisation.

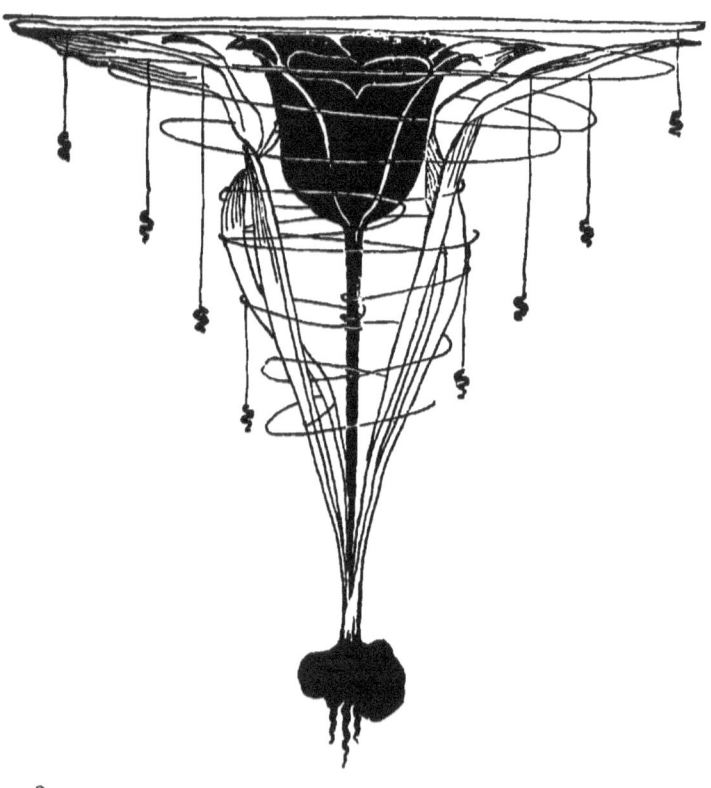

CHAPTER 5.—AN INDUSTRIAL DIALOGUE BETWEEN MR. ARCHIBALD PUSHINGTON, M.P., AND MR. THOMAS TRUDGE, TRADE UNIONIST

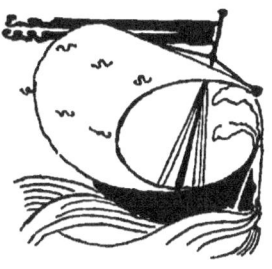

In the last two chapters I have dwelt upon the remoteness of the problems of Art and its education from the problems of the workshop and its re-construction; let me point a little to the reasons of this.

I once tried very hard to bring Mr. Pushington and Mr. Thomas Trudge together. Not from Quixotic motives, but from a mere love of fighting. There were a few questions I wanted to hear them argue out, for they had both heckled me with problems, and made a sort of mental middle man of me. But I could not do it. Mr. Pushington merely shrugged his shoulders and said, " *que faire* ! " Mr. Trudge laughed, and knocked the ashes out of his pipe with " You bet ! " So I was obliged to become an imaginary Dragoman to them, and dish up the questions in occasional and alternate scraps.

" Next time you see your friend—what's his name—Trudge —of whom you talk so much, just put him a few straight questions from me," said the Member for S.W. Kensington. Ask him where all this Unionism is going to end. Ask him how an industry is to be conducted without the employer of labour who has been specially trained for it. Ask him whether he, as a free Englishman, has no sense of right and wrong in the matter of compelling men to work according to a definite rule laid down by a Union whose action is constantly hampering and endangering trade. Ask him whether he would like his standard of comfort lowered by having to accept the wage of the German, or what he would do if it were a choice between that, and going out of work altogether ; or, better still, ask him what he would do if I closed one of

49

the Sky Sign factories, like Lord Fitzwilliam closed that pit of his, when the Union struck for a rise.

Respec-
tive points
of view
" Where the Unionism is going to end ? " said Mr. Trudge when we met a fortnight later. "That depends on the employers of Industry, maybe. I should think it will last longer than they, perhaps, when the score's totted up. His lordship seems to think that the Unionism is going to end in a general break up, explosion, demolition of things. He'd see it in a different light if he attended a few of our executive meetings. We've got out of the times of Tantiatopee and the canister of gunpowder. You've heard of the chap who used to cut the wheelbands of the Sheffield razor-grinders over night, and—well, he moonlighted the blacklegs, you see— it wasn't "moral suasion" in those days, not even stones at the pit's mouth. (That's what *you'd* call being militant I believe—eh ?) Well then the Unions were legalized, and we weren't locked up any more for combining, and we went in for numbers, oh yes, I know you'll say the sots and drunkards are pressed in, and though theoretically excluded are

Unionism practically welcomed, and it's a levelling down of the good men. But the levelling up is going on too ? When we've done what we want with our numbers, we shall raise the standard I suppose. Don't you think it isn't just the loafers that are our difficulty. It's they that bring the standard down, and it's they that are the employers' safeguard."

What we've got to do, now, is to fix what the socialist chaps call " the standard of life," and we shall do it, either by " minimum wages " or " limiting of hours," and this " standard of life " we shall, if need be, die,—or to put it less poetical and more striking—starve, for."

The
standard
of life
"It's very blind, blind, all this talk," retorted Mr. Pushington when the Dragoman dined with him on the following fortnight. " Really, though I consider he was very rash in saying it publicly, Lord Salisbury was quite right in calling the Unions a cruel organisation. It's a pity he didn't stick to his point. It is not in accordance with English national individualism, to which we owe our greatness, that a man should be deprived of the right of selling his labour where and how he pleases."

" I guess," answered Mr. Trudge, over our next Sunday pipe, " that that little remark about the Unions has lost the worthy Marquis a tidy few votes for his next innings. He'd have

50

done better, as the Boss observed, to stick to his point than
to try and explain it away—for at least you expect pluck of
a Tory leader. I see no cruelty in restraining one man's
action for the benefit of his fellows; if a man, by selling
his labour below a fair wage, is injuring others, he must be
restrained. Don't those cute lawyers of ours keep their
standard up :—little dodges of having one lawyer to tax
another lawyer's bill;—and your doctors, professional etiquette
and the minimum fee ;—and how about the quack ? I see no
difference between their case and ours; and, as for the
blindness, well—now, I think our sight may be as long as the
Boss's, least ways, I don't mind taking an average among
masters and men."

" But the future of Industry, the future of Industry," The
insisted Mr. Pushington over the port wine. " We must future of
Industry
hold the market ; the future of Industry depends upon our and
holding the market. The question is a world-wide question— strikes.
outside the province of Great Fadwell East. How can we
act abroad if we have our hands tied at home ? And what's
this living wage, I should like to know ; how can such a
thing possibly be defined : is it mine, or my footman's ? I
have no sympathy with such child's talk. To strike for a
minimum wage, in the teeth of foreign competition, drives
the trade out of the country."

" Now, look ye here," said Mr. Trudge. " When they tell
you that the d—d strike's done this, and the d—d strike's done
that, don't you believe them. Mark this!" and his strong fist
came ringing on to the table, and made the tumblers quiver.
" There's never been an industry that's been killed by
strikes ! But you tell them in return that there've been
many industries made by strikes, only they aren't always
managed by the same people."

" Then why do they talk of the Dock Strike, and the
decaying Thames Industries ? " I asked, " and the others, the
industry of the——"

" Faugh," said Mr. Trudge, as I was about to repeat the
string of Industries that were adduced by Mr. Pushington
as instances of disasters wrought by strikes. " That's
bagman's talk, black-coated gentlemen, counter jumpers.
The Thames Industries, I guess, were destroyed by iron,
not by strikes. Haven't they got less and less ever since
we gave up making wooden ships, and brought timber from

51

all over the world to the Thames ; why, of course, it's easier
to make the iron ships where iron is, and, you'll find where
an Industry goes to pot, it's because the conditions aren't
so good for its continuing there as in some other place. Moreover, the tonnage on the Thames has increased since the
strike. The Boss is quite right, though, the question is larger
than Great Fadwell East, but in more senses than one.
If Industry goes abroad, well, then, the labour movement
will follow it there. If trade is cosmopolitan, so is labour.
I wonder he didn't tell you, as he and his political
economist friends are so fond of doing, that prices must
determine wages. As if I didn't know the measure of those
acres of stock rooms at Sky Sign's, where we can store up
our heap of truck on reduced wages because prices are low,
and then sell them, to Messrs. Sky Sign's great profit, when
prices are high again. I'm d——d if I see it that way ; no,
no, we'll work less hours, so as to save the over production,
keep up our standard, and, by so doing, prevent that beastly
The living market of theirs from being glutted, as they call it. And he
wage wants you to tell him what the living wage is and how to
define it, does he ? Now look, man. I act for my wife and
the little ones, and that will define the living wage for me.
It's what I reckon will keep me just a bit better and tidier
than we've been before, provided I'm not injuring others
thereby. Mr. Pushington, and Mr. Pushington's footman,
and the docker, may define their own living wage in their
own way, every man must do that for himself. John Burns
hit the right nail on the head when he spoke square to the
engineers and said, ' If I thought you were going to spend
your living wage on betting, I'd go against the Eight hours.'
John Burns is a man, and I admire him for it. No, no,
every man must define his own, within such limits, above or
below, as shall prevent his either cutting other folk's throats
or picking other folk's purses, we get back in these matters
to the unit. Some men will spend their living wage in
beer—more fools they. Some are wiser ; it's the wiser we
may go with, they're the leaven, and they'll leaven the lump,
we get back in these things to the unit, see ? "

Mr. Pushington's individualism appeared to me as nothing
beside this, and the conversation acquired an interesting
piquancy when the abstract questions of constitutional
socialism were applied to the individualism of the English

52

artisan, with its bias towards a middle class and somewhat respectable ideal. We inevitably got back again later to the big underlying economic questions of unearned increment, interest and rent, but as the discussion was not a strictly economic one it turned to the more immediately practical question of how things were to be worked out here straight before us. I found Mr. Thomas Trudge almost as sceptical about the future of co-operative production as a panacea as Mr. Pushington. *Almost*, but not quite. There was a rock in the way somewhere, but he couldn't get its bearings. He accepted the principle, but talked vaguely of its practical working; and, in some strange and tortuous way, he got back again to the unit, and the standard of life. Taking the matches out of his pocket he lit himself a fresh pipe, then looked curiously at the box with a twinkle.

" There " said he, throwing it to me. " It's a bit gorey, they're General Booth's, but I like to think my matches aren't sweated. Wish I could buy them straight, and not only them but all other things, straight from them that make them ? "

In short, it was the great question of human relationship that lay at the bottom of his ill defined position, as, indeed, it lies at the bottom of most social and industrial problems, and, as far as I could define it, it seemed to plead for the necessity of our growing out of a system by which the producer is artificially cut off from the consumer. Still there was a rock in the way, and Mr. Trudge was unable to get its bearings. *Human relationship in industry*

Mr. Pushington, moving on a different plane, did not recognise the rock as a rock. To him co-operative production was a futility, a delusion, and, if Mr. Trudge's view was at once sceptical and optimistic, his went far beyond either pessimism or scepticism, it was cynical fatalism. *Co-operative production*

" It's been tried before," he said, " it's been tried before, and it has almost invariably failed. The masters have tried it, and the Trade-unions have tried it. Look at the miserable fiascos of Robert Owen, look at the failure of the Workmen's Co-operative Mining Company, and the Ouseburne Engine Works, and ever so many others."

" And why do thy fail ? "

" Oh, mismanagement, inexperience, want of discipline, I suppose ! "

53

"And do you think that workmen are likely always in future to suffer from these defeats?"

Mr. Pushington shrugged his shoulders. "Surely," he said, "we must allow something for *inherited capacity* and the reverse?"

"Quite so!"

I then turned to Mr. Trudge and spoke by the book.

"It's been tried," I said, "it's been tried before, this co-operative production, and it has almost invariably failed, the masters have tried it and the Trade-unions have tried it. Didn't all those experiments of Robert Owen come to grief, and the Workmen's Co-operative Mining Company, and the Ouseburne Engine Works, and ever so many others?"

"I can name as many as you," said Thomas Trudge.

"More, I've no doubt, but why do they fail?"

"Oh," said he, with entire simplicity and candour, "Mismanagement, inexperience, want of discipline, I suppose."

Inherited
capacity
"That's exactly what the Boss says," answered I, "only he added that we had to allow something for *inherited capacity* and the reverse."

"Quite so!"

"In that case you entirely agree, there's no difference between you whatever!"

"None," said Thomas Trudge, "except this, the question between us is by whom the *inherited capacity* is to be controlled and paid, and—well, I don't exactly know how to put it, how far it is to be allowed to act for itself or not. Is it to be controlled and paid by the producer, or is it as heretofore to be looked upon as a means by which the holders of capital are to use it only for their own, and not for everybody's advantage?"

"Theoretically, I suppose, to everybody's advantage *through* their own. But what then? How will it work out practically?"

"Oh I suppose by the producers making it so jolly uncomfortable for *inherited capacity*, that it will throw in its lot with the producers, rather than go skidding about by itself!"

He paused for a moment, as if to find words to adequately express his half formed conception of a collectivist as opposed

54

to an individualistic system of industry, and then said with emphasis, " I don't see why *inherited capacity*, which can always command, and rightly so, a good wage, or inherited capital, or inherited land, or inherited anything for the matter of that, should also control what the socialist chaps call ' the instruments of production '—'tain't fair and square ! "

This question appeared to me so difficult to answer that I, as it were, planked it down in front of Mr. Pushington between the decanters.

" You don't state the question fairly " he said, " it's an ethical one at basis, and what you have got to answer is, will your *capacity*, hereditary or not hereditary, continue or not continue to invent, and create, and organize for the community, if you deprive it of its reward. By taking away a man's power of obtaining wealth, title, honour, his power of transmitting these, and of building up a great family and a great name, you take away his incentive to industry, and destroy his utility for public service."

But Mr. Trudge replied, " Grant him honour, grant him wealth, let him have his full reward, good measure, ample, and overflowing, give him a title if he wishes it, authority if he wishes it, let his children bear a noble name, but do not give him, or them, the power of enslaving others by controlling the instruments of production for ever."

That, in slightly different words, was what Mr. Trudge said, and then as clearly recognizing, as Mr. Pushington, that the question was an ethical one at basis, he added,—

" If he really knew it, that imaginary man of yours, is it really honour you give him by according him the power to do dishonour to others ? "

Athens, he might have added, sent to Thebes a crown of olive, not shares in a copper mine. But then Athens had the sense of Beauty, and neither Mr. Trudge nor Mr. Pushington quite grasp what that means ; and Athens was cultured to this understanding by virtue of the slave class, on which her little civilization rested, but neither Mr. Trudge, nor Mr. Pushington would, at least, in theory, tolerate this for the modern state. Mr. Trudge, with his Union, is fighting against what his socialist friends call economic slavery, and Mr. Pushington, is he not an individualist, believing in personal liberty, and supporting every British movement for suppressing slavery in the Soudan ?

The reward of industry

55

The basis of the future state

The State that Mr. Pushington, and Mr. Trudge, and I, are constructing, is to have a different basis—*the machine and its productive power rightly organised for communal service*. Mr. Pushington has founded, drilled and organized, Mr. Trudge is to collect and gather together, perhaps even wrench from Mr. Pushington's hands, what he holds, and apply it for the common good, may be, and I— well, I was trying to find the synthesis between the two, when the conversation from the decanters got on to tendency—the unknown God. When we get to tendency we get fluid. Anyway, we got no further here, and I actually found myself quoting, with Mr. Pushington, the old rhyme of an old time, of the old byegone English aristocracy of the early Eighteenth Century. " The simple rule, good old plan, that they should keep who have the power, and they should get who can."

The distributive system

But we left the abstract question for a while, as I was still anxious to find out what the rock was that unconsciously troubled Mr. Thomas Trudge in his effort to get to the unit in human relationship, and its bearing on co-operative production. I came to the conclusion that the rock for the time being was the distributive system. This had to be weathered before the calm sea of collectivism could be sailed.

And the middle-man

The cry of the last two decades against the middle man has been, though a very formless, still a very real one. We cannot do without the middle man, the vendor, the hawker, the bringer to and fro of wares, but we can put him into such a position as shall enable his being controlled by the collective body of producers, and prevent his utilizing their labour primarily in his own interest. This, in fact, means that we can displace him from the false position into which he has often got, of keeping producer and consumer apart to further his own interests, instead of bringing them together to further theirs ; indeed, we have got to force him out of this position in order to again make possible this *human relationship* between producer and consumer, which is the all in all of good production and wise consumption. These bigger problems of distribution have not yet been grappled by the working classes, either in groups or through the State, and until they are, co-operative production must remain impracticable, except in special cases.

56

Co-operative distribution has been a success, because the workman has been both distributor and consumer.

We have, it would seem, to break the backs of these big distributive businesses, just as they, together with the workmen's organisations are breaking the backs of the big producers.

Mr. Pushington put it very shrewdly when he observed " It is quite a mistake to think that we producers are any longer the kings of industry ; it is the big distributors now— distribution pays much better than production."

The recasting of the distributive system is therefore a necessary preliminary to the full development, whether by groups of workmen or the State, of co-operative production. Men skilled in the methods of distribution, the *hereditary capacity* has got to be drafted into the co-operative workshop, and the market has to be studied, secured and made stable. What Thomas Trudge has vaguely called the " trade boycott," and the " middle class counter jumper," and the " pauper clerk," are all things that have to be attended to first, and he believes that the application of Trade unionism to the shop assistant, the paid servant of the distributor may bring us nearer to this end, but he doubts how far the middle class ideal of respectability, and distribution is essentially of the middle class, may be influenced by the trade unionist ideal of the raising and regulating of the standard of life. Of one thing, however, he is quite certain, and in this I entirely agree with him, it is a nobler thing to produce than to distribute, for the act of production implies imagination, whereas, distribution only needs wits and elbows.

But Mr. Pushington was quite shrewd enough to see that State appif there was any rock at all it could be blown up from propriaunderneath with modern appliances, and that by the State interest appropriation of interest and rent, the distributive difficulty rent would be solved, and co-operative production be no longer a problem, and that, moreover, the infernal machine was ready to hand in the system of taxation, daily slipping more and more into the hands of an enfranchised Democracy. But this was rank socialism, here were the sacred rights of private property openly scampering across a Kensington dinner table and showing their parts, so the goose, that laid the golden egg, of capital was evoked, and order restored. Mr. Trudge, too, was a little nervous at this sudden reduction of his position by Mr. Pushington to its logical conclusion, and he seemed anxious for some middle class, some conservative formula to help him through, as it were.

" Well, you see," he said "there be some that say there ought to be lots of little holders of land, and lots of little holders of capital, yet I don't see how that's going to better things, but only keep the present system going, and there be some that say there ought to be only *one*, the State, yet I don't see how that's going to work. Let's have one thing at a time, one thing at a time, please. For my part, I hold that the first thing we have to recognize is, the right of every man to the profit of his own labour. The question as to how far he has a right over other people's, is another question we can settle later."

" I'm not quite so sure about that " I said, " if we're going to be fair all round, besides, it may be cutting your own throat. Your building society now, and this house of yours, you have paid your instalments for it out of your labour, well and good, but when you die and leave it to Jack, and he sells it and knocks off work—he'll be living on other people's labour to the extent of its possession, how about that ? "

" You're a bit out there " said Mr. Trudge, " for it'll go to the ground landlord at the end of the lease, provided it stands so long, and as for Jack, he may shift for himself as I have shifted for myself.

" And the wife ? "

" Well wives are different, and so are orphans—something special will have to be done for them as such as I should say. You remind me of Henry George and his poor widow. They alays bothered Henry George with that poor widow, shoved her under his nose, and threw her at his head, and dropped her through his land nationalisation scheme, till at last he could stand it no longer, but pensioned her off, from the Queen down to Mrs. Gummidge, on £100 a year—premium on widows, eh ? but I see your point, I see your principle, we'll settle it when the time comes—one thing at a time, please ! "

While I was musing over this, and thinking how easy it would be for a Conservative leader to play upon Mr.

Trudge's sense of caution, he turned half mischievously and enquired—

"What was it the Boss said to you when you were to ask him if he recognised any right and wrong in closing the Sky Sign factory and turning five hundred people out of employ, even if he had no need to do it?" *The introduction of morality into industrial relations*

"Abstract questions of right and wrong must not be introduced into these matters," that was what Mr. Pushington said, "and as for the Sky Sign factory, just like Lord Fitzwilliam's pit, it is my property, and I am quite at liberty to do as I like with it : if I choose to close it, I shall close it."

"I don't want to go against the Boss's notions of private property," said Mr. Trudge, "and, as far as he's concerned, he may do what he likes with what he calls his own, as long as he don't injure other people, just as much as a man may do with his labour ; but when by abusing it he robs other people of the fruits of *their* labour, and inflicts compulsory idleness upon them, his property, which, let us say, for argument, was his own as long as he used it rightly, becomes a wasted trust when he abuses it, and my mates and I will have a Royal Commission on it—only, may be, we'll drop the ' Royal.' Ask the Boss, next time you see him, whether there isn't something in the Bible about a good steward— may be he's forgotten it, I'm afraid I have—but between you and me, Mr. Pushington *won't* close those works as long as it'll pay him to keep them open, and when it don't pay him any longer, well, then we'll have *our* little commission and see if it'll pay us, and what it's best to do—no hurry about that ! Look here, just you ask him if he'll show his books."

I did not ask Mr. Pushington to show me his books, because I should not have understood them if he had, but I asked him how far he considered that questions of morality and sentiment, and the abstract teachings of the founder of Christianity, for these, it appeared to me, lay at the root of Mr. Trudge's argument, should enter into the relations between employer and employed, or the conduct of the whole industrial system, and he answered—

"In personal relations they should be everything ; with business relations they should have nothing to do!"

To this Mr. Trudge a fortnight later said very little.

59

Indeed, I could not get him to pursue the subject, he merely remarked—

"The Boss acts up to his beliefs, and I've told you, when we strike for a rise, we strike on principle and not on Pushington, for all that he's a good sort, but if we meet in the House some day we shall be on opposite sides. What'll you take?"

CHAPTER 6.—
THE HONEST ENDEAV-
OUR OF TIMOTHY
THUMBS, TEACHER
AND HUMANIST.

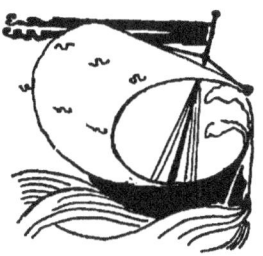

These economic speculations, and the war for the standard of life, have taken us far afield in our consideration of how the beauty of life is to be brought home to our producers, and of how their ideal of citizenship is to be shaped. But there is a little bridge over which we may pass, another path as it were to the same end. While the workshop is being slowly and surely reconstructed by the workman of the present, the type of the workman of the future is being curiously wrought by the elementary teacher. While Thomas Trudge is consolidating his Trade Union, his son, Jack, is being trained by Timothy Thumbs. Let us see how.

Timothy Thumbs is my very dear friend, and I owe him much. He is the head master, or, as the Board prefer to call it, the "responsible teacher" of the Grinders Street Board School, Great Fadwell East, that vast, grim, colourless building about a mile on after you get to St. Saviour's Church, and near Blooder and Stencks' Match Factory.

I want, in this chapter, to tell you a little of what Timothy Thumbs does in the way of technical education in his school, and the training of the young artisan in the fundamentals of the æsthetic sense, I want you to get to feel with me, too, that had we a little more regard for this æsthetic sense, we should get on much quicker in the solution of the problems of workshop re-construction with which these essays deal.

The sense of Beauty, or the æsthetic sense, which it is desired to train, I have ventured to define as follows :—

The power for wise use and enjoyment of natural surroundings and the human body in the first place, and, in the second, a similar power in the work of human creation—a noble building, a great picture, a refined piece of handicraft, national poetry and music.

Timothy Thumbs and the sense of Beauty

As Jean Paul says, we educate everything that will perfectly well educate itself, but for the sense of Beauty, which, above all other things, needs educating, we do nothing. I am certain that Timothy Thumbs has never read Levana, but his every iota of life proves him to be witting of this. The things that they will never get, either at home, or by the clemency of the Board of Great Fadwell East, such things, he says, my boys shall have from me ; and so he takes them out to the forest on holidays, when it might be supposed that a much-worked master would want to get away from the society of his tormentors for awhile, and covers the blank walls of the school with Walter Crane's heroic legendary and Randolph Caldecott's picture books. It is true that he also writes round to the great firms for their coloured advertisements—chocolate, boot-blacking, soap and mustard ; but that is because his power of æsthetic discrimination is not sufficiently developed. The good endeavour is there.

The dual life of Timothy Thumbs

Indeed, his is a curiously dual life. The one narrow, cramped, and forced upon him—at its acutest on the annual show day, when his children are crammed for the inspection of " my lords," who then enter upon their visible incarnation. The other, his real life underneath, the life of the born teacher : for this he gets no credit ; for this, neither the Board, nor the Rev. Simeon Flux, give him any esteem ; into this they never penetrate. Indeed, the Rev. Pettifer Jugge, the Chairman of the Great Fadwell East Board and the strong organizer of the Conservative party thereon, even regards it with mistrust. But there are some who value it, the Great Fadwell East Branch of the National Union of Teachers, to whom Timothy Thumbs is a tower of strength—they know his worth and honour him.

My University friends, especially the King's and Balliol men, are bored to death in his company : they see him as he is, a cockney, narrow, very narrow ; but then I always think their point of view is rather too refined, and you never expect much sympathy between one narrow man and another. I had a roaring medical from Caius once to supper, who told a lot of human and rather spicy hospital stories, and it was wonderful to see how Timothy Thumbs thawed, but the intellectual hauteur of King's and Balliol a little troubles him, and he objects to the *on principle* visits which the King's and Balliol men pay to Great Fadwell East.

He has done many notable things, Timothy Thumbs, but all in a cramped and purblind way, and all the notable things have been done by his real self in spite of his educated self. Indeed, they have not been asked or expected of him by the Board. The old boys' club, and the cases full of curios in the class rooms, and the regular contribution to the Art for Schools Association, whose prints make the walls pleasant to look on; the excursions out to Epping in the Spring, and the swimming competitions, with their rows of copper and silver cups, none of these the Board is much concerned with, they are not regarded as educational, but they are the " parerga " of life, into which he puts his whole heart. Pestalozzi, had he known him, would have wondered at and yet loved him; indeed, Timothy Thumbs, in spite of being a professional educationalist, is a born teacher, and full of the milk of human kindness.

Now, I want to state clearly, and hope you will note it, whether you be the King's and Balliol men, or ' my Lords ' of the education department, or the ex-governor-general of Bujoo, her Majesty's Inspector of Schools; that we are not giving this man a fair chance, we are handicapping him, spoiling him as a servant, wasting him as a man! Doubtless you will say, is it right that much responsibility should be put into the hands of a man who can be got at so small a salary, so low a price ? Isn't it much wiser to establish a great machinery, a system, and let the individuals conform ? I venture to think not. I venture to take into the account a little human enthusiasm ; and though you must feed your man first before you can expect it, I deny that this little enthusiasm is a purchasable article. This, too, I insist upon, and it is a question that burns into the vitals of our educational system, we must put a little more of the sense of Beauty into life. We must make our schools more beautiful, the lives and times of the masters more pleasant, the teaching of the little ones more genuine, the ideal more

63

human, more Greek, a little less commercial, less English. If we did this, we should not be so troubled with the valuation of our teachers in the monetary scales. It is not true that every man has his price—and there are other things to be reckoned with, questions of character, of sentiment, of the teacher's power of attraction.

Grinders Street Board School

Grinders Street Board School, in which you have cooped up Timothy Thumbs, is a huge, yellow-brick case, with windows in it, built in the choicest office specification style, and looking like a large, overgrown and ill-ornamented urinal; there is not a tree anywhere near it, and I do not think a blade of grass would grow there even as a weed, it has a sheet of brown gravel for a playground, and there are, not slummy, but dreary, melancholy, characterless streets all around it on every side. Nor is there a work of Art anywhere near it, or anything pleasing for the eye to rest on, for I do not call pleasing the statue of the great radical politician at the end of Horwark Highway. You know this hideous dummy. It stretches out a big, black, oratorical pump-handle to the Democracy of Great Fadwell East, but somehow the Democracy are not moved by it, nor do they count its erection as among the good actions of the late Mr. Jonathan Blooder. I don't think the children ever heed it. They are wise, and it certainly does not inspire with respect the æsthetic sensibilities of the match girls, for I *have* known them solemnly trail out before that statue and spit upon it, radicalism or no radicalism, because the late Mr. Jonathan Blooder docked a penny a week from their wages in order to erect it. It is strange this sort of thing, is it not ? And yet we know that Blooder and Stencks' is the best appointed factory in the world—always employs British labour! However, Grinders Street School is near here, as you turn to the left by the factory.

You will notice, if you please, especially those who are seeking to inspire a soul into the corporate life of London, that I am quite correct and definite in my description of this place, and its name, yet I doubt if you could recognise it from any other; it is just the Grinders Street Board School, and its next neighbour, as you may know, is the Mudford Road Board School, and the next one after that the Cramwell Alley Board School, and so on. They are all alike, as like as one wasted pea to another, no chance, no hope for one to assert any individuality of its own. There

64

seems to me to be no reason why this should be so.
Indeed, there seems to me to be every reason in the world
why it should not be. If the corporate life among us is to
come to any noble fulfilment, to blossom into any outward
expression of the enjoyment, the Beauty of life, it can only
be by a right recognition of the individuality of the different
educational centres: the fulfilled corporate life must begin
in the school.

Why should the upper class boy be trained, not at "the The "Public" School
public school," but at Clifton, Eton, Marlborough, Win-
chester, and this mean something definite and lasting to and the
him ; but the artisan boy be trained at no place in particular, "Buard"
but just at "the Board School." You shall never tell me School
that individuality is a purchasable commodity. I want to
see Grinders Street mean something quite distinct from
Mudford Road, and be something definite and lasting in the
life of Jack Trudge's younger brothers. There is no reason
that this should not be. Let the school become a little
more the centre of communal life, bate a little of the system,
allow a little more for the individuality of the masters. We
English of to-day are always so forgetful that it is the men
that do the work and not the machinery.

Now I have asked for a little more recognition of his
individuality, and in exchange I am going, in my next
chapter, to ask Timothy Thumbs something in return, but
I wish here to plead also for two other things in our elementary education—a little more *continuity*, and a little more
recognition of the sense of beauty in the life of our schools, our
teachers, our teaching. Let me explain what I mean more
fully.

By a little more *continuity*, I mean the connection of the The need for more continuity
life of the elementary school with the life of the district in
which it is situate, the life of its inhabitants, and this
continuity, further, through the connection of the little
citizens after they leave, with the school in which they have
been taught. We must establish school traditions, but the
establishment of school traditions should not be left to the
teachers single handed. It should be furthered, helped,
and subsidized by the Boards. Let each school have its
clubs and its trophies, its old boys' meetings, and their
names, and their prowess, and their affections, and their
little heroisms and successes recorded on the walls and in
the books of the school. The school-house should be a

65

store-house of the lives and characters, the individualities of the little citizens. You need not tell me they are too young —that the teaching of the Board School ends too early, and the impression will go. It is just that period in our life which is most impressionable, when the mark on the wax is most firmly implanted. Look back at your own life ; have you not a more vivid recollection of the events of your existence between eleven and fifteen than between fourteen and eighteen ? I think most of us have. There is also this to be remembered, the little artizan boy is much more impressionable than the public school boy, because his life is more real, he comes daily and immediately into contact with the facts of life. He is not waited on by servants, he knows the fire is there to warm the hearth and cook the breakfast, he early has a grip of what is meant by labour, he is not diverted by too many toys, nor artificially shut off from the sorrows of the world ; all this makes the teacher's impression more possible, more valuable to him.

The need for more encouragement in the sense of Beauty

As to the recognition of the sense of Beauty : what we are trying to stimulate is *the power for wise use and enjoyment of natural surroundings and the human body in the first place, and in the second a similar power in the work of human creation,—a noble building, a great picture, a refined piece of handicraft, national poetry, and music.* It is unreasonable to suppose that we can accomplish all this in the Elementary School, but we can there lay the foundation for it, if we go the right way to work. We can give our little citizens a fundamental understanding of the principles of colour, mass, form, line ; we can teach them to enjoy a landscape, and respect their own bodies ; we can train the ear to music, the eye to loveliness, the heart to citizenship. I shall be told that much of this is already being done in the infant school by the Kindergarten system. True, but it is not nearly enough done. It is done much too much as a system, it is not carried through into the teaching of the boy, it is done without sentiment. There is no continuance of it into the teaching of the higher grades, and it is not connected with or related to life. The little citizen, in short, is not trained to feel the significance of it.

There is no reason, except that of cost, why, in every Board School, there should not be a miniature workshop for carpentry and modelling and painting, a forge, a lathe,

66

and a drawing room. There is no reason, not even of cost, why there should not be an occasional tree in a school playground. When they built Grinders Street School, on Lord Brewster's building estate in Great Fadwell East, the Board's architect specified for the clearing of the site; three elms, some fine planes, and two superb cedars were consequently cleared. There is no reason, except that of cram and Her Majesty's Inspector, why a large proportion of the teaching should not be out in Epping Forest and in the swimming baths. All this stupid, stunting, stultifying, lore, of books and figures,—what do we want with it, what does it serve us? "The poor little street bred people that vapour and fume and brag," that is what it produces for us. Let us have something more real, more substantial, more nourishing to life.

Can you expect much of Timothy Thumbs, my friends? Isn't it wonderful how, for dear love, and in sheer spite of circumstances, he does so much? Yet whatever of this living, concrete, human teaching towards the sense of Beauty, he gives, it is out of himself, and not out of the clemency of the Board of Great Fadwell East.

I suppose it was some tradition of the little Hampshire village in which he and his before him were trained—ages ere the School Board days, and when the Rev. Pettifer Jugge was still in Heaven—that made him once in my hearing give his lads a most exquisite lesson, yet quite unconsciously, in the sense of Beauty and the fundamentals of citizenship. It was by an old oak in Wanstead Park: he was telling his boys how foolish people were to cut down trees—jerry builders, and architects, and irresponsible ground landlords, and such like.

"I'll give you a rule," said he, "for you to remember when you get big. *Never cut down a tree if you can possibly help it!*"

And then followed some other talk about the many oaks that good Queen Bess, wise and thoughtful woman that she was, had planted. "And here, Jack, as we're about it, look at that flower—d'ye know what it is?" Not Jack, how should he. "Well, it's a periwinkle, it came out of a garden once and is wild now; and see—I'll give you another rule. *Never pluck a flower unless there's a very special reason for it.*"

At this he bent down, and, though to me, for a moment,

A lesson from Timothy Thumbs

67

he seemed to be himself transgressing the rule he had made, he picked the periwinkle and gave it to Jack. But Jack saw the special reason, and the look with which the flower was given explained the paradox.

It is the unconsciousness and the sympathy with which these things are done that makes them so valuable, and I believe that what little talent for drawing, designing, construction, there may be in Jack, he has had drawn out of him in this way. Timothy Thumbs has no knowledge whatever of design, you may take my word for that, yet by sheer mother wit has he distilled the elements of designing ability into a few of his boys. Among other happy ventures he has told them to decorate the margins of their books with "scrolywigs," as they called them. He had a copy of a page of the Book of Kells, he once begged of me, hung up in his school, and, by way of employing listless fingers, told the little citizens to ornament their books. Of course these scrolywigs were very ugly and blottesque, but theirs was teaching on the right lines. Technical Education in the Board School if you like.

Grimness

When you travel by rail into the "great wen" from South, North, East, and look out of the window, you see miles of chimney pots and tiles, and every now and again, as who should say peppered in among them, and towering over them, are these brick boxes of Board Schools. They have so very evidently been dropped into their arid plots of asphalte by a central Board, that is quite out of sympathy with the grey blinded life of the community about them, that it is not surprising they, in their turn, look bewildered, are out of sympathy, muddleheaded. The impression they give is one of grimness. "We are all admirably organised" they seem to say, "but what exactly is it we are trying to do?" There is a purposelessness about the aim—we need not call it the ideal—of their education. *It is grim.*

As far as I can see, neither the Progressive, nor the Conservative, leaders of education, seek, in any way, to mitigate this grimness, both seem afflicted with the cumbrousness of the organization. Even the Rev. Pettifer Jugge, pachydermatous as he is, is oppressed by this. Both aim at politics in education, rather than at education in politics. The Progressives are in too great a hurry to educate citizens for the purpose of the franchise—as if how to vote was the end of education! the Conservatives are

68

too anxious about the old order, forgetful that they are letting the spirit of it slip. The Rev. Pettifer even holds that Great Fadwell's salvation lies in the Athanasian Creed, but he finds some difficulty in explaining it to the other members of the Board.

I call the educational aim of either party grim. This grimness is inevitably reflected by Grinders Street, and Timothy Thumbs, though he callously conforms, and often with bittterness of heart, to the Board's Progressive or Conservative wheelwork, unconsciously keeps his æsthetic sense for his boys outside the work in life for which he is paid.

I am very fond, when I have a spare hour on my hands, in East London, of going down that endless, dreary road, to the Grinders Street Board School, and into the grim, gaunt building to visit Timothy Thumbs, and take him unawares at his work. He little knows, and would be the last to believe it, that I never come away from one of these visits without a new idea. Everything is ugly, the street, the building, the walls, the method, the organization, the discipline ; but Grinders Street Board School has just one element of redemption in it, it has the little citizens of the future, and the personality of the man who, notwithstanding all the trammels about him, is shaping their destinies to a more human end. When I see this, I pull myself up, and say, " There's hope in the Democracy yet, in spite of all the ugliness."

Another lesson from Timothy Thumbs

I took Timothy Thumbs unawares once in this way, and brought back a new idea that had a deep underlying significance for me as to the relation of the sense of Beauty to life ; indeed, summed up, in most perfect manner, the highest technical and artistic education possible for the school. It was a warm summer's day, and the air was redolent of that stuffy, pungent, leathery smell that you get among the boots and brick-dust of Grinders Street. A little citizen, who had asked permission to leave the room, and was cracking nuts like a squirrel in the playground, led me up the steep stone staircase to the room where teacher was, and was just going to introduce me when, peeping through the door ajar, I saw my friend with a box of brown and coloured chalks in either hand. Wondering what he was about, I signalled the little citizen to be silent, and we both stood out of view.

Timothy Thumbs was talking to his class about keeping their hands clean. "Now," said he, "see here. I've got something nice for you. But first I'll see whether you're fit to have it." (Forty little citizens looked up with blank faces in expeétant astonishment,—what on earth was teacher going to do?) "I want you all to lay your hands out, *so*, on the desks." (Seventy-nine little paws—for one was in a sling—were spread out, all grimy and curly, on the desks.) "Ah! I see; very black, those of yours, Tom Smith, shan't have anything nice for you; and yours—well that's better, now look! I've got two boxes full of chalks, see, *chalks* to draw with, like *so!* In *this* box, they're all dirty chalks—same colour as your fingers, Teddy Brown, but in the other box they're all full of nice colours, blues and greens, and yellows and violets—look at that!—all the colours of the rainbow, there!" (and a big but undulating arc slowly dawned upon the black board). "Now you may all draw if you like, but all the boys with dirty hands will draw with the dirty chalks, and all the boys with clean hands may draw with the bright chalks." (Instantaneous and uneasy rubbing of seventy-nine curly hands upon corduroys). "No, that won't be much use! There, *you* may have some colours; and *you*, and *you*, and—oh! no, dreadful! dirty chalks for *you*." (Furtive studies of comparative cleanliness from desk to desk among the forty little citizens).

And so on till ten of the forty only were voted clean, and the æsthetic sense of the remaining thirty was quickened into life by a longing for bright colours and a craving for clean hands.

My little citizen growing impatient, we entered together, and though the others were too much absorbed in their new accomplishment to notice my entry, Timothy Thumbs was a bit confused, and wore a look of half pathetic, half humorous apology. "I must get the little devils clean!" it said. And he got them clean, too, in a week.

Now I did not so much care about the cleanliness, but the recognition of the æsthetic sense—that was a master-stroke, a touch of genius. Yet Timothy Thumbs is no genius. Where does he get all his ideas from, do you think? He is not a man of much imagination. Why just here, he has that one crowning mercy in his work which all we designers and architects are starving for, which Mr.

Pennyworth would give his right hand to secure; he comes into direct contact with his material. We are all steel without flint; but for him there are the little citizens of Great Fadwell East, they flash out the ideas for him. Could we not leave him a little more freedom in the details of his Art and Craft of Education, look upon him a little more as a man, a little less as the cog in a machine?

It is curious to watch how our English constitutional ideal and the control of the purse by Plebs works in Education. It is the political see-saw without the inspiration of a great measure in the policy, or a great personality in the administration. There is the Buff Board and the Blue Board, each with its capacity for party pugilism. Buff Board has won a triumphant election on the cry of " Ware Rates ! " and straightway the policy of retrenchment begins. The rate drops visibly. We reduce the salaries, we knock off the teachers, we keep appointments in suspension, we overcrowd the classes to the limit, we cheapen the bricks. The rate is down as low as Buff ingenuity can get it, and Blue wrath is rising on the cry of re-construction. In fact the impossibility of doing education properly on a falling rate, an increasing population and an enlarging franchise inevitably asserts itself after the second year, and slowly and surely up goes the rate again. Then comes the next triennial election, and Blue Board comes in with a triumphant majority and the cry of " Ware Rates."

What a miserable people we are. Here we have done a magnificent thing in starting a system of national education, and we let it go to waste like this, for want of—what? Why this : a little more regard for the beauty of its details. The whole thing has got to be made more interesting, more human, more free. We appeal to the pocket only, we do not recognise the other finer, human qualities in our electorate, our teachers, our children. Will the little citizens do the same do you think, will they vote on the cry of " Ware Rates ! "? I venture to think that a little more training in the fundamentals of the sense of Beauty, while it will help us greatly in the reconstruction of the workshop, will help us also to the wiser shaping of our Ideal of Citizenship.

Meantime we have got to knock the shackles off Timothy Thumbs. As we tighten the ties of government, and, whether for good or evil, get nearer to socialism, so it behoves

The Electorate in Education

71

us all the more to guard the individuality of our men, for on this all great government in the end must rest. Perhaps I am prejudiced in his being so near a friend of mine, but I plead for a little more freedom for him, a little more of the light and colour of life, a little more recognition of his individuality. You politicians and staticians, whose view of life is so wholesale, and who are apt to forget its little humanities, I ask you to untie his hands a bit. You have a fine servant in him; tell him frankly that you entrust to him the training of the young Democracy, and leave him a little freer to do it. I plead for Timothy Thumbs!

CHAPTER 7.—THE HIGHER ASPECTS OF TECHNICAL EDUCATION AND THE ELEMENTARY TEACHER.

BEING AN ADDRESS
TO THE SOUTH
ESSEX TEACHERS'
ASSOCIATION.

In this chapter I want to ask something of the Elementary Teacher. It is a very practical, rational, sensible thing, I think, and there is just a little bit of an ideal thrown in with it too, which those who think ideals will not pay, or in the language of the Elementary Teacher won't earn grants or get certificates, need not take.

I am seeking, throughout these essays, to show what appears to me to be the relation of Trade Unionism to the re-construction of the workshop, and what should be the attitude towards Trade Unionism of those of us who are seeking to pioneer education in the workshop, for the purpose of re-construction. I want to ask the teacher also to look the problem of social re-construction in the face : he has his share of it to effect, and his share of it is a great one.

He is wavering at present, and thinking that it will be better for him and for education, in which, if I measure him rightly by Timothy Thumbs, he is genuinely interested to dignify the profession of the teacher by placing it more abreast with the other professions—church, bar and medicine ; but in this I think he is mistaken, and I hold the point of view an old fashioned one. For my part, I think he should turn rather to Unionism, should enter more into the spirit of the labour movement, should let himself be represented on its councils, and try to help guide its educational destinies, and should recognise his own National Union of Teachers as among one of the leading Trade Unions in the country. What I ask of him is, that he shall, in these matters, take up a fresher, newer, larger, point of view.

F   73

Aspects of
Trade
Unionism

The principles of Trade Unionism, as at present understood, are broadly these. Combined action among the members of any trade, for a larger share in the benefits accruing from that trade, whether in the shape of increased wage, or greater margin of leisure, or, in other words, more control over the implements of production. These benefits being presumably limited in quantity, it follows that it may also become the Trade Union's business to regulate them so as not to waste or destroy them. This, some of our younger workmen's Unions do not as yet fully recognise. There are further two aspects of Trade Unionism, the militant and the constructive. When the Cabinet Makers Alliance, or the National Union of Teachers, or the Amalgamated Society of Engineers, or the Royal Institute of British Architects, or the Boiler Makers Union, fashion laws among themselves for the regulation of the wage or fee that their members are to receive, their Trade Unionism is constructive ; but when any of these bodies try to force a registration bill through the House of Commons, or do a little picketing for young boiler makers, or young architects, or pupil teachers, or Jew cabinet makers, their action is militant. I do not say that it is wrong, all I say is, that in order to make the construction possible, the militant work has probably got to be done. I admit, too, that each Union has to be judged on its own merits, and on the question whether or not it is doing the work it professes to do. What I ask for, however, is that we shall, in the first place, regard Trade Unionism as a whole, and recognise the need for a large, comprehensive understanding of it, and a similarly dignified policy with respect to it.

The
Teachers'
Trade
Unionism
versus
Profes-
sionalism

Of the teachers, in especial, I ask, and of Timothy Thumbs, too, that they make it their policy to throw in their lot with Trade Unionism rather than with Professionalism, and I would like to offer it as a suggestion to them, that there are certain things they are striving for, which they will only obtain through doing this.

I would put it to them thus : You want to raise the social status of the teacher. You can do this in two ways, and of these the one is much more important than the other. The one way is by enlarging the salary, the other way is by enlarging the man. Combine to enlarge your men, combine to force Boards and Departments to enlarge your men, to give them more responsibility, more independence. It is a thing worth striking for. Remember Blake's

74

proverb of hell, and *strive with systems to deliver individuals from those systems.*

I have a grim recollection of being invited by Timothy Thumbs to the Annual Inspection at Grinders Street. Her Majesty's Inspector for Great Fadwell East is the ex-Governor of the crown colony of Bujoo, in the South Pacific. He is a fine, manly, somewhat caked and crusted British soldier, whose brilliant service in India and ten years government of Bujoo was considered by "my Lords" as qualifying him for guiding the educational destinies of the little citizens of Great Fadwell East. The examination I was privileged to watch was in grammar, and the veteran of Bujoo wrote upon the board:

Another lesson from Grinders Street

> "*If any man says he knows more than he does know, he who says this does not know what he says.*"

That was to be parsed, picked to pieces, noun, adjective, verb, and so forth. Timothy Thumbs looked at me, and I back again to him, and a nervous shudder went down my back, for fear I might be called upon as a referee. I felt that I did not know what I should say, and that I certainly could not say what I knew, and that though I had mastered the nouns, adjectives and verbs in my boyhood, I was never able fully to discriminate between the prepositions and the adverbs. After the trial, Timothy Thumbs said laconically—

"Isn't it rot, all this grammar; the boys would be much better doing bench work or singing, don't you think?"

The furtherance of Education versus the checking of Organisation

I did think. I thought that the mental training was needful, but that there were perhaps other ways of doing it than by parsing the ex-Governor's knowledge. But what struck me most about the whole Departmental visitation, was that the Inspector's object appeared not the *futherance of education,* but the *checking of organization.*

I submit that we have got beyond this, and that in its place we want more individuality, and more expression of personal character, in school, in teacher, and in child. Strike for this individuality, I say. It is that that will give you your better social status. I mean it quite literally. Combine, and go on strike for it. We all respect a man more for his extra independence than for his extra £30 a year. Far be it from me to begrudge Timothy Thumbs his extra £30 a year; I think he well deserves it; but a little extra freedom would give him much extra dignity.

I would like, however, to show yet further, more nearly

the bearing of this Technical Education problem, this problem of Workshop Re-construction, upon your teachers' problem of the raising of the status, and the shaping of the Ideal of Citizenship for the young artizan, whose future is in your hands. Let me first put you a question. What do you think it means underneath, this recognition of the need for Technical Education? Why, a return to that other side in teaching that, for the last three hundred years, and since the decay of the mediæval guild, has been more and more neglected. Neglected, to begin with, by the scholarship of the Renaissance—we all of us love Roger Ascham, but some of us think his *School-house* is too grammatical; neglected, in the next place, by the pedantry of the eighteenth century—we all of us love the "Spectator," but some of us think that his exquisite speech would have been the sweeter for a little feeling in a great workshop life, to draw experience from, but this, the eighteenth century could not give ; and neglected, finally, by nineteenth century professionalism and machinery. We all of us respect those who have given the touch of greatness to the life of Church, Bar, Hospital and Laboratory, or who have brought the century its inventions; but some of us think that we have not had enough individuality allowed us, whether we be tied to an education code or to a weaving machine. Far below, and in its greater sense, the Technical, the more concrete training of our children, reverts to an earlier age, when we English people expressed our greatness, not in our books and our professions, but in the productions of our hands, and in our workmen's organizations, when we built Canterbury, Westminster, Wells, and Montacute, and when we acted "As You Like it " in the open-air theatre at Penshurst.

(margin note: The Elementary Teacher must line up with the producer)

I want you teachers to feel the bearing of this movement for more concrete teaching—in other words, the educational side of my problem of workshop re-construction—upon your problem of Professionalism and Unionism. It is the training of the young producers, of the future citizenship, that you have in your hands ; you have to shape the Ideal in the wax : if you wish to be abreast of the times, throw in your lot with the producers, and you may yet see the image cast in gold.

(margin note: Higher aspects of Technical Education)

Let me essay some little further definition of these higher aspects of Technical Education. The Greek word τεχνη means an *art*, and so we shall do well to limit the word Technical to anything that is produced in Industry, in Craft, or in Art, *in which the hand either works alone or in*

76

conjunction with the brain, in contradistinction to any subject in whic͡h the brain works alone. Or, stating this more epigrammatically, and in its educational bearing, *teaching in the concrete, as opposed to teaching in the abstract.*

Accepting this as a working definition, we might profitably consider what the points of view with regard to it, respectively, are of the master of Industry, the workman, and the Elementary Teacher, and, moreover, what they severally take Technical Education to be. I would put it thus : The master of Industry, no doubt, quite rightly, from his point of view, says—give me more able workmen, the foreigners are beating me in my market. I want better tools to work with. It is true we should not directly teach trades, but give me something that will better enable my hands (he is a manufacturer, and, therefore, makes things with *hands !*) to perform the work I want of them ; that is what *I* mean by Technical Education. The workman, also, doubtless quite rightly from his point of view, says—I would rather not be made a better tool of, and if Technical Education is to mean that improved boy labour is to bring down the rate of wages, I object altogether, not to mention "squat," or the doing of supplementary dilletante work, thereby depriving skilled men of their market. On the other hand, if my boy Jack can be better fitted for some line in life (anything but my own) than he is at present, there may be something in it— if I can get it cheap. The teacher, as yet, cares for few of these things, he does not much understand, or much sympathize with, these positions, nor has he yet grasped the bearing of Technical Education upon his own craft. Technical Education to him, so far, means extra evening jobs, and wonderful new vistas of certificates.

If you have gone with me so far, you will have discovered that the view I am asking you to take, of Technical Education, is a wider one than this ; that, indeed, it is bigger than can be possibly covered by any certificate, or expanse of certificates. Let us return to our definition, and see if we can construct on it something that shall meet the wants of employer, workman and teacher. I decline to go with the masters, and regard Technical Education as a means of improving the producer in the fashion of a tool; I decline also to go with the workman, in his mistrust of Technical Education on this ground ; but I hold that Technical Education must, in the end, be for the artisan, and be conducted by him ; it primarily concerns the workshop.

77

As for the teacher, he has to study it in its elements, and in its bearing upon the children—the young artisans of the future. So I would press this point with you, that Technical Education, inasmuch as it is *Educational* as well as *Technical*, has not only a commercial, but a moral aspect also, its object being to make a man, not a better tool, but a completer man. It is an aspect of the training towards the new citizenship, it must be regarded, not as a thing apart and by itself, but as part of the existing system of education, with which the elementary teacher is connected; it must, in fact, be conducted concurrently with primary education, and grow out of it.

The Parable of the Cabinet

I would like to state the case to you in the form of a parable. You know those beautiful cabinets in the South Kensington Museum, made by the Italian and Flemish craftsmen of the Eighteenth Century, they are among the finest pieces of workmanship we posess. There is, first of all, a stately structure with solid doors, delicately moulded and carved. In the centre is a golden key; you turn it, and open the doors, when, within, you see the panels still more beautifully wrought, sometimes with colour and gesso, and a miracle of workmanship in the many drawers and recesses. The best work is within. You may fitly store your treasure in this cabinet, for the lock is a good one, and the shrine is worthy the most sacred relic you can yield it. And, as to the interpretation of the parable, well, I think a child is won by concrete teaching. Things visible, palpable, tangible, appeal to it first, then it must feel, and finally it can understand. If the cabinet is our symbol for the concrete teaching, expressed through its many forms of handicraft, the higher knowledge is within, stored in some particular drawer; but the teacher holds the golden key. If it were not too much of a conceit, I would go further, and suggest how each drawer, each technical form, is the vehicle of some educational treasure: in this drawer, so delicately mitred, is the creative sense—shall we not teach the child how things grow and hold together—in this drawer, with its carved arabesques, is the "sense of form," more valuable to the little one than a rule-of-three sum. Here, again, is a drawer, inlaid with tinted ·marqueterie, you accept its glittering challenge, and find the sense of colour, surely of some service to the little purblind infant of Mudford Road; and here, in a neglected corner, a panel on which is graven some forgotten subject in ancient history,

78

you open and find the historical conscience of a nation and its life expressed in handicraft. And there is still one innermost recess, the secret drawer to which the others seem to lead, and there, within, is the perfected citizenship.

These are none other than the elements of that higher knowledge with which, in Technical Education, we have to deal—form, mass, light, colour, creative force, reverence and historical tradition in work and national development, the sense of beauty, and so forth, all you have to do is to unlock the cabinet and, as I say, take your part in the problem of workshop re-construction.

Technical Education has this other human, moral side to it, *Human* *and moral* as distinct from the commercial; and as soon as the *side of* elementary teacher sees this human and moral side, and *Technical* divests it of the stuff it is so often wrapped up in, sheets *Educa-* *tion* of statistics, and backs of blue books, and old class registers, the publications of societies, and the records of trade machinery and organization, it will come to be no longer a dull and dreary subject to him which he ought to take up because the times demand it, and to win certificates, but a subject of fascinating and absorbing, because of real educational, interest, and because it supplies just that element which is wanted in the curriculum of elementary teaching. *Handwork*, as well as *headwork, teaching in the concrete*, as opposed to *teaching in the abstract*: not grammar, not the knowledge nor the didactic modesty of Bujoo.

And what have you, for whom this is written, to do, to attain the object? I say you must unite and form yourselves into definite groups to understand, and then to make for what you want; you must find out the technical needs of the district in which you work, you must watch the way in which the monies to be devoted in each district are to be administered, and you must act in this with the Trade Societies; it is your province to guide education. To sum all up in a word, you must be militant. The teacher always has been militant, from the days when he founded Bologna and Paris, Oxford and Cambridge; or, again, when he led the new learning of the Renaissance through Colet; or again, when he passed the Education Act through Forster.

In this newer movement, the possibilities of being more real, of teaching more humanly, are being opened out to us. We are given a better chance of preparing better the men of the new order, of shaping their Ideal of Citizenship. It is men we want to produce, not tools, not machines.

79

Technical Education, as I conceive it, implies the widening and broadening of the limited man. It occurred to me, as I was pondering these things for you, how the old Psalmist hit off that moral and human element in the modern movement: when he expressed, unconsciously, his own educational ideal : " That their sons may grow up as the young plants, and that their daughters may be as the polished corners of the Temple."

CHAPTER 8.—ON THE TEACHING OF DESIGN, AND ITS BEARING ON WORKSHOP RE-CON-STRUCTION.

We will leave the little citizen and his teacher for awhile, to return to him later. In the present chapter I would like to discuss the well-worn subject of the application of design to Industry. Jack is being trained in a shop whose pro-ductions are abominably bad, as far as design goes. Is it any use teaching Jack this, and, if so, are we to try and improve him, or are we to wait for our re-constructed workshop to do it ? Can we teach him design ?

It almost sounds like a paradox to commence a chapter on the teaching of design with the proposition *Design cannot be taught.*

I would, however, do this, and qualify it with three other propositions, to the effect that *there are certain conventional arrangements in various materials that can be taught;* that *technique can be taught;* and that *to those who have the designer's gift, a certain other something may be taught, and that something is—style.*

Of these four propositions the last is the most important, and upon them we may construct a chapter on the Teaching of Design. The practical Englishman will, however, ask for yet another, and I would state it thus : *the crux with us is how to combine old traditions with modern conditions.*

At the outset, however, it will be well to define what is meant by design, and to clear away the vague meanings usually attached to the word. *Design is that element, in any Art or Craft, by which the whole hangs together, first construc-tively, and then æsthetically.*

I am afraid that this definition will upset many a " design class " established on government grants. Yet it is none the less absolute. You cannot teach design as a thing in itself—as an abstract noun. It must have reference to something : a building, a table, a dress, a jewel, a lamp, a book-page. I knew an enlightened gentleman once who had what was called a " design class for boys," and his method of teaching design consisted in making the boys draw conventional patterns, from natural forms, into circles, and copying Walter Crane's picture books. After a few years this began to pall, the boys dropped off, it seemed to tell upon their nerves; many hundreds of circles had been described, and the Walter Crane picture books were thumbed to tatters.

Those boys were quite right; they have my entire sympathy. They instinctively felt what their teacher could not see, that, what of design was teachable, could only be taught by creating, in material, that technique; *the complete power of the Craftsman over his material* can only be achieved by learning the values of material, and, much more still, that style, *the expression of a man's own character, and its relation to the age in which he lives,* was only teachable if the designer's instinct was there.

The value of design classes It follows from this, that so much of design as can be taught, viz.: *technique* and *style,* cannot be taught, or only very superficially, in classes. Certain branches of technique, that may be dissociated from the primal underlying element of design, may be; but, at its best, a class is not a good place for acquiring them. A class cannot be creative, it must run in regular appointed grooves; if it is an evening class, it is necessarily superficial, unless it is very small in numbers, *i.e.,* limited to three or four pupils; it must lack the personal element essential in the teaching of design, it can rarely see a piece of work through the various stages of material, and it does not tend to bring out a man's own character. Such classes as are valuable are life classes, classes for drawing—up to a certain point,—classes for the use of the hands, and so forth, for children; but design classes are not good, they cannot really lead to anything, and that is what many, who harbour the belief that a revival of English design in Industry is possible, through classes, will, in due course, discover. For the present, the class epidemic continues.

Let us for a moment look at all the work in which the element of design enters, that is turned out in London. It is divisible into three groups. I venture upon a statistical shot thus:

Design in modern productions   1 per cent. The work of eminent designers.

2 per cent. The work of businesses of the first order, that have, or have had, artists at their head.

97 per cent. The commercial article.

Keeping on the windy side of the libel laws, I would instance my per-centages thus. In the first group I would place the work of men like Bodley, Norman Shaw, Alfred Gilbert, and a few of the painters who are not only painters of exhibition pictures, or the sculptors who are not merely makers of busts. In the second group I would place the work of firms like Morris and Co., William de Morgan, Benson, and one or two others, where considerations of design are regarded as having prior claims to those of commerce, and where, as my friend Mr. Pushington would add, " The business often goes to pieces." In the third group I put firms, good, bad, and indifferent, from Messrs. Gillow's, Doulton's, Farmer and Brindley's, down to Moses Maple and Company, in Curtain Road.

These, be it noted, are, in each group, only types of many others which courtesy, or delicacy in matters of advertisement, would prevent my mentioning. The productions cf groups *one* and *two* we may leave to take care of themselves, the productions of group *three* we want to improve, and the youths trained under each of the three respective heads we want to do something for, from the pupils of the architects and sculptors, down to Thomas Trudge's bench boy at five shillings a week.

There are, as I say, certain things that they can all learn in classes, but there is a much more genuine way in which we must help them, if we are really to make all-round workmen of them, and that is *to combine the teaching function with the workshop function.* Of this I shall have more to say below, suffice it that I need only re-state what, to the educationalist, is a truism, that the Art of the teacher is always the same, whether it be in the teaching of drawing, or of cabinet making, or of Latin verses, or of football, it is two-fold, first human, then technical ; and this great educational rule applies as much to that portion of design that can be taught as to anything else. First you must win your pupil's heart, then you must train his fingers. Until we bring our teaching into the workshop, we shall neither make it human, nor shall we make it technical.

Need for combination in the teaching and workshop functions

The creative artist, if he has studied the social and the educational aspects of design, would endorse this, and soon be able to point out the reason why of success or failure ; but then he is not asked ; and one of the great difficulties with which we have to deal, is the effort persistently being made by grant-giving committees, to run Art and Science together. They are a sorry pair : they don't understand each other, and, as a rule, the scientific horse is on the near side. I have never known an instance in which a practical artist has been told off to superintend the work of laboratories, and draw up syllabuses for heat, chemistry, or electricity. The science men wouldn't like it, and, perhaps rightly so, they

Customary English methods of encouraging design

would write long and conclusive letters to the papers; but it is a common thing to expect the supervision of the artistic teaching in our schools from the science man, and I find he seldom feels any compunction in undertaking the duties. This, on the face of it, is absurd. The lasts are twain, and each cobbler must stick to his. It is quite certain that, unless a practical artist is placed at the head of the system of teaching, any scheme must inevitably fail. When I say fail, I mean in the larger bearing on Industry, in its creative outcome such as design in furniture for the East London Cabinet Makers, or design in glass for the blowers of Whitefriars, in stone and clay for the masons and potters of Lambeth, or in architecture and building for the hundreds of young apprentices and "assistants" who "draw" the designs for our streets, while the Chief attends to the light and air, organisation, correspondence, commercial travelling, and generally the more lucrative work of of the "and surveyor" part of the profession. It is easy enough to start little classes in practical work, and make a condition that lectures in design are to be given with them; on paper it looks perfect, but I do not see what it is to lead to in practice; I do not see how it is really going to touch the workshop.

New suggestions In the excellent report issued some time ago for the London County Council on the Technical Teaching of London, a valuable suggestion was thrown out as to the need for the appointment of a *Normal Art Master*, to superintend and direct the whole of the artistic teaching of the Metropolitan Schools. The suggestion was admirable, but the title! and the insinuation implied in it! I cannot think what devil of Philistinism could have syllabled so terrible a title. The functionary in question has not, to my knowledge, been yet appointed—let us hope he never may, if he is to be thus labelled. We do not want a Normal Art Master, a creature dressed in paper, with the Board's brand on his collar, and a chain round his ankle, but we do need a man, a creative artist, a *higher producer*, who shall gather together all the educational threads that hang unconnected from the different schools, polytechnics and educational bodies in London, and shall have some knowledge of and sympathy with the workshop. His functions should, I think, be two-fold. He must start as an artist from a purely *a priori* point of view, and, if I may so state it, this point of view must be his own capacity as a designer and craftsman. This capacity must be recognised in him, and must not only be left free to continue, but he must be encouraged

84

in his creative work and tied to no apron strings of Boards. In the second place, he must endeavour to correlate the artistic teaching of the Metropolis, and, in so doing, get all the best designers and craftsmen in London, who do anything in the direction of public teaching, to co-operate with him.

Whether this be possible remains to be seen ; at present it appears problematical. Funds are there, but they are too grudgingly doled out to make possible any genuine grappling with the educational problems indicated above. The flesh is willing, but the spirit is weak. It is questionable, too, whether such an appointment should be made by a municipality, and, whether it does not rather come within the province of a functionary not yet himself in existence, to wit a minister of Arts, whose duties shall also be two-fold, first, to look after the leading educational appointments that deal with the teaching of Art and Craft, and then to care for the country's public monuments.* We have a minister of Education now, it would be interesting to know whether he would welcome a colleague who would undertake this higher portion of his duties, and certain others not yet performed by anyone.

Our next great educational stumbling block is the sub-division of labour. How are we to teach design, that is to say, what is teachable of it, namely, *technique* and *style*, in its direct application to material, when the pupil has no chance of coming into contact with the whole of his material; when one portion of it is made in Birmingham, another in London, another in New York ? It is the workman we want to teach, yet this stumbling block implies that the workman is, and can only be, cognizant of a twentieth part of his work. How to teach him the remainder is the question, and our educationalists, bound by the Act, say, " Oh, he shall learn the remainder by State Aided Technical Education," that is to say, *in an evening school.* {.marginnote}The bearing of sub-division of labour on the teaching of design

This may be all right in the teaching of science—I am not an expert and cannot say—but every practical artist knows that is is futile in Art. That same design, that element by which the whole hangs together, and which can only be got at by intimately relating it to the parts, that same design demands a man's best, necessitates his comprehensive, attention.

Here, then, we have the economist's bugbear of the sub-division of labour brought directly home to the artist,

* The destruction of the Old Palace of Bromley-by-Bow, of which I spoke above (p. 18) is an instance of what would not so easily have happened had there been a minister of Arts. It would have been his duty to look after this historic building.

the *higher producer.* We cannot shirk it, we have to face it straight. But does it not force two reflections upon us that may help us in our subsequent action ? That, on the one hand, the position of the professional designer must inevitably be brought into much greater prominence, and that, on the other, if design is to enter more fully into Industry, it must be cheapened. At first sight this is a paradox, the two things incompatible, but when we think it out more carefully, we shall not find it so.

I have said, not only in this chapter, but in a previous one*, that the head designer's study must be comprehensive. He has to do with *that element in any art or craft by which the whole hangs together, first constructively, then æsthetically*; he may specialise on sculpture, on architecture, on jewellery, on stained glass, on tapestry, though perhaps I may be forgiven if I say that the more architectonic the art in which he specialises, the more capable will he be for comprehensive designing. That is by the way. But he must, before all things, have a grip of design, in its application to Industry, all round. In the apt expression of Edward Thring, as applied to teaching generally, he must be a " Jack of all trades, and master of *one.*" And this very sub-division of labour, which reduces the workmen, who are engaged on the production of a piece of work, to a hundred disconnected and unin-terested units, forces the comprehensive designer into prominence. He has to pick, and select, and arrange, and supervise, but, before all, and on the strength of his experience of men and craftsmanship, he has imaginatively to create.

The comprehensive designer, as long as we have an industrial system, based upon individualistic production instead of the craft guild, and conducted with minute sub-division of labour, is, and must be, at a premium. He is the only person who, in the province of industrial art, can, in any big way, create and originate.

On the other hand, I affirm that design must be cheapened if it is to enter fully into modern Industry. I can imagine the employer of labour, my respected friend, the member for South West Kensington for instance, as he reads this, bowing to himself, and saying deferentially:

"That's exactly what I've always said. We cannot place artistic work on the market if we have to pay so much for design. The public won't take it."

But Mr. Pushington and I always have little differences on these matters, and his view of cheapening varies from

Rate of payment to the "trade" designer

mine. His view of cheapening is illustrated by the following
case in my own experience. Mr. Pushington is not in the
silversmiths' line, so he will not mind my telling it. I was
asked, some years ago, to purchase for a friend a silver salver,
and as I had not, at that time, started the making of silver
things at my own workshops, I was advised to go to the
leading silversmiths' in the City. I went, and stated that I
had £20 to spend, and might I see some salvers. Dish after
dish was brought out, each worse than the first, utter
degradation; all that one could say of them was that they
were shiny. In despair I said:
"Well, I'm afraid the design of these is all so bad; would
it be possible to have one,—just a plain square, with no design
on at all! just a simple sheet of silver, with the ends turned
up?"
"Oh yes, sir, certainly!" (a salesman never fails you.)
"And I suppose it will make some difference in the
cost!" (You should never ask leading questions of a
salesman.)
"Oh yes, sir, undoubtedly.
"How much?"
Enquiries were made at head-quarters as to what the
difference in the cost of a £20 salver would be if all design
were omitted, and the answer came back:
"About four shillings!"
Now the designer's remuneration may be arrived at by a
simple rule-of-three sum. As £20 is to four shillings, or
less if we omit the retail per centage, so is the amount spent
for general commercial and "other" purposes, to the wage
paid to their designer for his work, and its execution, by the
notable firm of Messrs. ——, but even Mr. Pushington,
liberal as he is, would admit that there is something wrong
here!
Still we say design is to be cheapened. I do not,
however, mean by cheapening the further cutting down of
the wage of the already underpaid hack draughtsmen who
do the sketches for the big firms. I mean by it, the training
of the workmen to do it themselves, and giving them the
opportunity of doing it themselves. This is a matter of
time, the division of labour stumbling-block is in our way,
and the logical carrying out of this means nothing more nor
less than the break up of the big workshop. I believe,
however, that the disintegration of the big workshop is
inevitable in all branches of work where the element of
design enters, and the inevitable substitute for it is a
federation of small workshops, in other words the "guild,"

or co-operative productive society. But of this I shall speak later.

Our next educational stumbling block is the attitude of the workman himself.* His point of view, though not sufficiently clearly formulated, is quite straightforward. He is suspicious of education that is taken up by, and presumably, therefore, in the interest of, the masters of Industry, and he is opposed to anything in the nature of half teaching, which means that the masters may be able to employ partially trained youths, who have had a superficial grounding in evening classes, at a lower rate of wages than would be paid to thoroughly trained workmen, and he hates "squat" with a bitter hatred. He, further, is very sensitive; doctors and lawyers could not be more so, of trenching upon the work of other Unions not his own. With this point of view I fully sympathise, only I do not regard it as a permanent one. It is primarily defensive, and, I believe, in course of time, the growing responsibilities of the Trade Unions to the Industrial development must reverse it, and lead to a more far-sighted educational policy, emanating from those with whom it ought to begin, namely, those who are creating with their hands, rather than those whose first consideration is the yearly dividend or profit.

The primary difference between, let us for a moment call them the Trade Unions of the middle ages, and our own, is that the former were, among other things, directly responsible to the community for the goodness of the work produced; consequently the education was in their hands, and it was done through the workshop. This, as I said above, we have to aim at, to revert to. To me it seems that every possible endeavour should be made by municipal bodies to induce, or where possible, to oblige, the Unions to take over educational responsibilities. This, again, is a matter of time, and the Unions have to win their wage-battles first, and become directly concerned in the management of the Industry before they will trouble themselves with its betterment from the productive point of view. As to their present regard for design, as here discussed, it does not concern them. The practical problems of Industry, and the practical problems of Art, are at present too disconnected. But they will not long so be, and then their bearing on each other will be direct and all absorbing. Re-construct the workshop's social conditions, and the improvement of its design will inevitably follow. What our municipal bodies and councils have immediately to do, is to seek for any group of

---

* See Mr. Thomas Trudge's point of view, page 33.

workmen, and by workmen I mean, men working with their hands, who are in any way interested in the educational problem, and give them every possible support.

But to return to the question of the *teaching* and the *workshop functions.* I have always insisted that in their combination lies the only right method of imparting any subject, which implies the application of Art to Industry. The South Kensington system has reversed, and must continue to reverse, this method, and the clause in the Technical Instruction Acts against the teaching of trades, will make to the same end, and be an obstacle to the County Councils. However necessary this clause may be, I believe that practical experience, or rather necessity, will upset it. It has certainly, in many instances, already been got round. The whole question of the application of design to material is involved in it, and points to the need of its abolition ; that question is a technical question, of which the framers of the Act, with all due deference to them, knew nothing. This clause is the difficulty felt by everybody who is anxious to make industrial teaching effective. It is an obviously reasonable clause, but it postulates a competitive system. It is reasonable that the State should not aid one producer at the cost or to the exclusion of another. If, however, we conceive of a developed cooperative system, the clause stultifies itself, and the difficulty vanishes. Meanwhile we have to face it.

It is being got over by various people in various ways. Some draw a line between the theory and the practice of a subject, some at the sale of the commodities produced, where teaching involves production, some deliberately ignore it, and just teach, regardless of any qualification. Perhaps this is the wisest plan. In some cases, notably in industrial Art, you cannot teach at all, except by just teaching what may directly be termed a trade. The question as to what is a trade, is often only a difference of degree. A trade, without venturing on a definition, I take to be something at which somebody can earn a living by the skilled work of his hands, but in Industrial Art nothing is worth teaching unless a living can be got by it, and you cannot teach it unless you go direct at your material. Theory, drawing on paper, elementary training,—all very good doubtless, but then they are all off the point, as far as genuine training is concerned, and the point is, the *instant technique* of the artist workman.

I take a case. In Birmingham they pride themselves on their enamels. Their enamels are really very bad indeed,

Teaching and workshop functions again

as everybody who has made a study of enamels, and most of the best Birmingham men, too, know quite well. We want, with all respect to the Birmingham enamellers, to improve these enamels by means of technical education. How shall we set about it? By giving lectures on design with the black-board? By comparing a good enamel with a bad one, and talking about colours to people sitting on forms in gas-lit class rooms? No, I say; and I can imagine a shout of derision from Benvenuto four hundred years away, as he looks out of his workshop, furnace-bar in hand, and jeers at the young Birmingham artisans at the evening certificated classes. No! by standing over the workman as · be bosses his metal plate, and paints on his flux; by showing him where to leave and what to give; by telling him not to be so beastly clean when he peppers on his colours; by just flinging in a pinch of *rosso* here so as to give an accent, and pushing him out of the way in the nick of time at the furnace's mouth. I know of no other way. But is that, or is that not, teaching a trade, according to the Act? And will the Council give us a grant for that? It's the only way we can beat the Germans, you know! And if we really want to learn how to do better enamels, we had better give up the pretence of trying to do it in any other way for the sake of the Council's aid. It is quite certain to me, that we shall never have a genuine system of industrial Education until we do teach trades. The real question, I think, is to whom are we to entrust this teaching, to the masters of Industry, or to the men? This question leads us to my last proposition, which was, that *the crux with us is how to combine old traditions with modern conditions.*

Old traditions and modern conditions   It is generally admitted now, I think, that the work of the past—the work produced in this country, for instance, up to the end of the Eighteenth Century, and the advent of the industrial revolution, may be taken as a standard for the joint excellence of design and workmanship in English Art and Craft, and it follows from this, that the conditions, under which it was produced, were favourable to its production. Published records, such as the Government Commission of 1888, on the London Livery Companies, are at hand to prove this, though, to the artist or expert, a study of old work itself is sufficient proof. Now, the traditions of the past, under which the good work throve, were, broadly, two, *the tradition of the Guild* and the *tradition of the Workshop.* The tradition of the Guild implied a co-operative and exclusive system, and a corporate responsibility among the producers to the community for the goodness of the work produced. The tradition of the Workshop implied a storing and handing down, from generation to generation, of old methods of workmanship, in small workshops, every craftsman's direct interest in the work of his own hands and his personal responsibility to the Guild for it. It followed necessarily from this, that technical and artistic education, in our sense of the word, was implied in the workshop teaching; there was no educational difficulty outside the workshop, and divorced from it.

In place of this, we have, at the present day, a competitive and individualistic, instead of a co-operative system; large workshops with machinery and sub-division of labour, instead of small workshops; and in place of the mediæval Unions of highly-skilled workmen, the militant Trade Unions, loosely leading armies of partially trained workmen with daily less opportunity for their thorough teaching. It seems almost grotesque to require that old traditions shall be applied to these conditions.

I do not only, however, affirm that this must be done, if the past standard of excellence is to be arrived at, and, what is much more important, maintained all round; for the prestige of a strong man working for a small public, may keep going, for a while, work that is quite worthy of the Guild tradition of old; work such as Mr. Pushington delights in personally, but would call "not strictly an article of commerce"; but I affirm that it is actually being done, that old traditions are actually being re-applied. Slowly and deliberately we are, not returning to the workshop of the middle ages, for return is impossible, but making for a re-construction of the modern workshop from within. Any new regulation of industry, any reduction of the hours of labour, any joint action, whether of Governments or of Trade Unions, that bears on the interaction of trade between various countries, any development of Unionism to regulate Industry, from the craftsman's point of view, any development of the Co-operative Society, or embryo Guild, bring sus nearer, not to the mediæval workshop, to that we can never return, nor should we seek to do so, but to *the conditions that made possible the production of its commodities.*

In the militant Trade Union, and the productive Co-operative Society, we see the elements of a revival of the two traditions of the past, the *tradition of the Guild,* and the *tradition of the workshop.* Look further for a moment—imagine the Trade Union, at the end of its fighting tether, the maximum wage won, and the master of Industry reduced to a position in which it is no longer to his interest to conduct the Industry as a personal venture. The responsibility for its development inevitably devolves upon the Trade Union, and, the only practicable machinery for its continuance, the Co-operative Society. Then imagine further a development of the co-operative principle and groups of workshops formed with traditions of their own, stored up for the future of the workshop, instead of for the head of the firm and his family, and we have a close approximation, only on a larger scale, to the two mediæval traditions. It is at this point that our genuine system of industrial education will be effective. In short, as I have before suggested, we must convert Mr. Pushington's great house, Sky Sign and Co., into a sort of Industrial Partnership, whose future is vested in its producers, not its entrepreneurs, and we must utilize the sum which our public opinion extorts from his munificence, not for the purpose of swelling big polytechnics, but of teaching in the workshop. Next time I see Mr. Pushington, I will ask him, in all seriousness, whether he has sufficient confidence in the men, of whom he speaks so highly, and appears so proud, to entrust his capital to their management: or is it to be Argentines, or Ottomans, or American rails. The question is rather a delicate one. We shall see !

Mr. Pushington, who very courteously consented to look through the proof sheets of the above, says I am quite right, the crux is as I put it, but that we cannot combine old traditions with modern conditions. My answer is that if we are to bring back design into the workshop, we must. We shall see. Time, and, may be, the Trade Unions, will determine many things for us, of which at present we reck little.

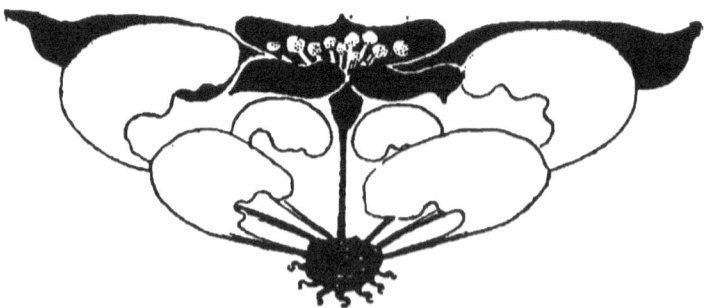

CHAPTER 9.—UNIVERSITY EXTENSION AND THE WORKSHOP. A PROBLEM AND A POLICY.

We have now, however superficially, regarded a few of the problems of workshop re-construction from within; how they appear to Mr. Thomas Trudge, and to Mr. Pushington; we have considered the bearing upon them of the Technical School, and of the newer ideas of Technical Education, and we have taken an all too hasty glimpse into the little creation, that is going on, down below, of the citizens who are to form the knowledge of the future. There appears to me, however, another way, by which the re-construction may be guided, and the Ideal of Citizenship shaped. This other way is through University Extension—the grafting of the humanistic studies upon Industry.

I was invited once, by the Oxford Delegacy, to give a course of Extension Lectures at a new centre in Berkshire —to break ground for them. The centre was an artisan centre, and as it happened to be near Mr. Pushington's place, and he was to take the chair at the opening lecture, he invited me to stay. The Rev. Simeon Flux was among the guests, and being one of the leading lights of the London Extension Society, he was, of course, asked to speak, which he very kindly consented to do.

It was decided, therefore, that the rector of Great Fadwell East, as an eminent Extensionist, should introduce me and "the movement" to the audience, and that Mr. Pushington should take the chair and sum up.

The Rector opened the ball. It was evident at once that the meeting was going to be a success. The audience felt that they were in presence of a great speaker: the speech was short, and it held their attention throughout. He explained the Extension movement,—what it had done, what it was doing, what it was going to do; the Extension movement grew and multiplied as he was speaking about it; it began to creep and spawn, and swarm, and overflow; it became a mighty, national, nay American, world-wide, oceanic, movement; it depressed you with the sense of its vastness, its strength, its genuineness, its modesty. In that moment you felt, had University Extension been on the political ticket, and the ballot box at the door, every man in

93

The Rev.
Simeon
Flux in
oratio
obliqua

the hall would have plumped for the Extension candidate. Then the Rev. Simeon struck another note—Religion. The Extension movement, he said, was fundamentally a religious movement; it brought the Religion of the new age, the Religion of culture, of light, of sweetness, of free thought; we had come to the end of the time when dogma was the first essential, even doctrine might be treated more or less symbolically, and was not so important as every man's individual thought; the Extension movement was the *rubric* of every man's individual thought. "I," said the rector, " admit it frankly, I believe in *Being*—it is a nobler thing to *Be* than to *Do*. In that moment you felt that the Church was on the right lines, that the great churchman was with us, that this was the man for the pulpit, this was the man to put new life into the Church; that if the Rector of Great Fadwell East said this, what more could one wish, and the Extension movement assumed the form of a sweetly reasonable crusade—it was winning, suggestive, convincing. Then once more the Rector changed the note. The Extension movement, he said, was the movement of Democracy, it was one of the forces of the new civilization, it was for the people, for the artizan. The Universities at last were coming to the light of day; they were stretching out the hand, they were stepping from their seclusion, and bringing education to the poor. "I am a University man, myself," he cried, "and can speak. We were an aristocracy at college, we kept the light, and the privilege, and the learning to ourselves, but that is all gone by. We recognise that we have duties as well as rights, and we are trying, in our humble way, to fulfil those duties. In speaking to you to night, I feel as if I am doing a duty to my college. I owe everything to my college, and I love my college as I love my wife." In short, you felt, as you listened, that the Universities and the people had somehow got divorced from one another, though *how* was not clearly explained, and that the Extension Movement was bringing them together again, that the mountain need not try to come to Mahomet any more, and that Mahomet had at length come to the mountain, and so forth, and that in the University Extension Movement, as the Rector said, to close with, there was only one class—neither upper, middle, or lower, " but the class of earnest thinkers in Democracy. We can learn citizenship in the Extension movement. Let us all be earnest thinkers in Democracy."

94

You might have heard a pin drop while all this was going on, and when I rose to give my lecture, I felt like a beetle suddenly uncovered in the light, and anxious only to hide myself. What my lecture on this occasion was about, I forget, nor does it matter. It had to do with the local Industry. My lectures, as a rule, appear on the posters and in the Extension papers as lectures on Design, but they really have very little to do with Design, that being a subject, as I have before pointed out, which one cannot lecture about; but they deal with what I would call the humanizing of Industry. Their method seeks to be different from the ordinary Extension lecture, often but a hackneyed boiling down of the latest academic ideas for the consumption of the middle-class, and their attempt has been to get men, especially workmen, to feel the relationship between their work in life and their mental development. In short, they make for the higher aspects of what in these essays I call *workshop re-construction*. Suffice it, that, whatever I said on this occasion, fell very flat after the Rev. Simeon's speech, and the title of my lecture, in which I foreshadowed the course, may be nameless.

After me, Mr. Pushington summed up. He spoke very quietly, and very sensibly. He thanked me for my lecture, and though he begged to differ from some of my statements, as to the necessary conjunction of industrial life with a movement for Education, he did not, he said, wish to bias the minds of the audience with anything he himself thought, They must judge on these matters for themselves at the end of the course, which, whatever one might say against it, certainly promised to be interesting. Then he thanked the Rev. Simeon Flux for his admirable speech, and the ideal of culture he had set before them ; and, though he was not himself able to endorse all the Rector's views, he hoped none the less that they might be stimulating to all present that evening. It was evident that Mr. Pushington did not sympathise with the Rector's ebullient and comfortable optimism. Mr. Pushington's speech, though less moving, appeared to me more dignified. He avoided the Trade Union problem as he would fire, and insisted that all controversial matters should be kept out of educational questions. As to the relationship of the University to Industry, he said that, in his opinion, the first duty of a University was the cultivation of learning within its own precincts, and that the sending out of teachers into other

Mr. Pushington's armed neutrality

parts, though doubtless admirable, was, after all, only an incident in its development. "To every one," Mr. Pushington said, "Education must be a personal matter. I hope you may all be personally gainers by what the lecturer has got to say to you. I wish him every success, I wish the Centre every success, and shall hope to help both to the best of my ability."

The evening was on the whole an admirable one, and the local secretary was radiant; but when it was over, and we were driving back in the brougham, Mr. Pushington, the Rev. Simeon Flux, and I, somehow formed a triangle, of three sharp angles equi-distant. We were all out of humour with one another. Mr. Pushington lit his cigar, leaned back in the cushions, and began the attack. Somewhat cynically, but very kindly, he made for me. What was I driving at—what did I want to do—where was it all going to end? The Rev. Simeon Flux chimed in too— he did not smoke, and so, perhaps, he was a little less cynical, and a little less kindly—where, indeed, was it all going to end? Why did I not point more to a mission, a modern mission—he, surely, had given me the lead. Why throw away academic culture and method? Workmen, before all other men, surely needed this—the scheme of my course was too vague, and, at the same time it was narrow. Why speak so exclusively to artisans, and hint at controversial topics—" You did not exactly talk Socialism," he said, "but you played with fire."

Then Mr. Pushington turned round and rent the Rev. Simeon Flux—.

"Oh, as for a little Socialism," said he, "that's neither here nor there, we all do that—but I can't understand how you, Flux, can possibly talk as you do about University Extension. The thing has got no more bottom to it than this cigar. The thing wouldn't go on for another six months here, or in Fadwell, if it weren't for my credit. The teaching is superficial and scrappy. It has not, and cannot have, any real relation to working men, and as to taking up the line you did about the duties of the Universities, I really think it unwise and dangerous to speak so. It is University Distension from the University's point of view," said Mr. Pushington, and he tossed his cigar, which was a bit dry, out of the window, and lit another.

The Rev. Simeon Flux was about to defend himself, when Mr. Pushington continued. "No man is more liberal than

The triangular duel on the policy

I, as you know perfectly well, and I try to show this by practically supporting the movement, but as to calling it *religious* and *democratic*, or looking at it in any way as a great educational force, it's all nonsense—it's all nonsense!"

But here I sought my opportunity. "What is the movement, and what do you want to make of it? What is your policy, I mean, of University Extension, in its relation to the artizan and to Industry? We are all agreed that the University's first duty is to encourage learning in its own precincts, but what is the object of the Extension movement among workmen. If it is to send out teachers at all, and be a force at all, it must have a policy. What is your policy, gentlemen?"

They both chimed in at this, but as each sought to lay down what appeared to him the right attitude of the University towards the great forces of Industry, the other invariably differed, and in the end, our triangular duel elicited no policy at all. They were both agreed, however, in criticising my lecture. They thought it off the point—in fact, a failure—and considered that, though I was strictly impartial, and gave no opinions upon burning questions, I introduced subjects that were irrelevant, and could not be justifiably called Extension subjects.

Out of the seventy or eighty artisans and elementary teachers that were present, some six had come up to the table afterwards and asked to join the Students' Union, and to have my advice as to their reading. So I held the lecture a success, and on my report of the Course to Oxford subsequently, the central office endorsed my opinion, despite either Mr. Pushington or the Rev. Simeon Flux. I may mention that these six students have, for the last three years since the lecture, been regularly reading and discussing the problems there dealt with, and one of these men is now the labour member on the District Council; but somehow they never ask Mr. Pushington to take the chair at their meetings, and the Rev. Simeon Flux is forgotten.

Now, I am prepared to grant many of Mr. Pushington's points, and also one or two of Mr. Flux's, and I will endeavour here to lay down the outlines of what would seem to me to be a policy that might guide the work of those of us who are seeking to make more real the action of University Extension among working men. I am not here going to consider the rightness or wisdom of the University's taking such a step. The step having once been taken, I shall assume that the University, whether Oxford, Cambridge, or London, has decided for the best.

Outlines of the policy   The outlines of my policy I will place then under the three respective headings of *subject to be taught, method of promoting teaching*, and *qualification of teacher*.

In the first place, we have to regard *subject* in its two broad divisions. There is the general culture, the more harmonious Education of the artisan, and there is his special education for the direct improvement of Industry. It would seem, at first sight, that the former is the province of the University entirely, and that the second must be accomplished by the men themselves. In other words, while it is for the Universities to take the lead in a humanistic movement, it is for the producers of Industry to control, and consequently to educationally guide, its better

Subject to be taught   production. Though good for purposes of generalization, this needs qualifying. It will be admitted, I think, that by far the larger portion of the work of University Extension, whether among artisans or not, would come under the first of these two headings, *i.e.*, general culture, and hence, even, if incomplete, of humanism, but it is not as yet admitted, nor even fully recognized, that a large and continually increasing portion of the special, the technical, the industrial, contains in it the humanistic element, which it might, also, therefore, be the University's function to guide. For instance, those subjects, which in the large sense of the word, would be comprised under the term Art, as applied to Industry—direct production for the ennobling and beautifying of life. On the other hand, there are many subjects coming under the second heading, the special, technical and industrial, in which it is admitted that the University alone must lead, *e.g.* such subjects as come under the heading of purely scientific teaching—Science in its application to Industry, and the study of the laws that regulate the production, distribution and consumption of wealth.

Now what may we consider that the future wants of British workmen will be, in regard to these two divisions of the subject? To determine these will help us to forecast, in great measure, the future of the Extension movement. Like the middle classes, for whom it at present mainly exists, workmen need humanism, though their more direct contact with the fundamental facts of life often give this need a different direction.

As the movement for the shortening of the hours of

98

labour, or in other words the lengthening of the margin of leisure, gains ground, they will need it, and express the need of it more. But unlike the middle-class, they will seek for something more special, more technical, and more applicable to the second side of the work of University Extension, the special, technical and industrial. It would be out of place here to consider the reason of this, but one point concerning it should be held in view. The want of higher and more special teaching in Industry is being universally felt, because the apprenticeship system, which formerly supplied it, has broken down ; but we, when seeking to supply it, have to keep fixedly in view that the apprenticeship system can never be superseded by any system of higher teaching through University or Technical school—that since the apprenticeship system is essential to Industry, it must be reconstructed in the workshop, but that the province of the University, by leading the higher teaching, might be to assist indirectly in its reconstruction.

As regards subject, therefore, we may, I think, assume that the workman will need humanism, will need the special, scientific, technical studies that bear directly on Industry, will need the productive and creative that induce to humanism, and will need something that may guide him educationally in the reconstruction of the industrial system, in as far as it trenches on Education. These we may term his needs, and those needs, it is not unreasonable to suppose, he will ask the Universities to help him in supplying.

Let us now proceed to our second heading, and consider, not how far it is the province of the University to supply them, but assuming that University Extension is prepared to make an effort to supply, at all events, some of them, what should be its *methods of promoting teaching*—its policy considered constructively. To begin with, it must be a cardinal point with us to work through existing organisations. We should seek to understand the labour movement, that is revolutionising and reconstructing Industry, and in doing so we should recognise that here, in nineteenth century England, two distinct movements are going on simultaneously—the humanist and educational, the aftermath of Renaissance England, and the social and constructive, a retrospection to the mediæval England that made the Craft Guilds. If the changing and militant Universities may be said to represent the first, constructive Co-operation, and militant Trade Unionism may be said to represent the

Methods of promoting teaching

99

second. The University Extension of the future should aim at a fusion of the two, a dovetailing of the culture of the Universities into the constructive solidarity of the new industrial system.

Now there are two main channels through which we can approach the workman, the one essential for the present, the other for the future, of University Extension; the one is workmen's organisations, the other is the elementary teacher; Thomas Trudge and his union, and Timothy Thumbs and his school.

Much has been already done to bring University Extension in touch with workmen's organisations—witness the Co-operative Societies—but much more has yet to be done. There are the Trade Societies, the Unions, the Clubs, the Benefit Societies, and the various machinery, co-operative or otherwise, forming amongst workmen, for the regulation of Industry, its production, and its distribution. These the Extension movement has not as yet made any attempt to meet on a large scale. It recognizes them, but only in isolation. It has formulated no policy as yet for recognizing them comprehensively, and, as it were, *because* of their existence.

Assuming the rightness of formulating such a policy, it would not be inexpedient, I think, for the University to recognise the representative principle more fully, by inviting representation on some Federal Council of Trade Union leaders to discuss the prospects or the methods of organising Education among working-men. If these bodies once got to feel that the Universities looked to them, rather than to the masters of Industry, to further an educational movement among workmen, the present inertia of the Unions towards Education would assume a very different attitude. The prestige and educational authority of the Universities is strong enough to do this, without involving them in any of the controversial difficulties of Industry.

Granting, then, that it is right for University Extension to work through, and connect itself with, labour organizations, an opportunity is already at hand, in which a connection of this kind will be invaluable for the furtherance of its work. The County Councils have granted funds for Education applied directly to Industry; the Universities have, in many cases successfully administered these funds. It is not unreasonable to suppose that the Trade Societies will come forward, as they have already in several instances, and insist upon the allocation of these funds, conformably

Marginal note: University Extension and labour organisations

with their own ideas of Industrial Education. University Extention would do well, it seems to me, not only to be prepared for, but to anticipate this. The Universities should say to the Trade Societies, "We recognise you as having responsibilities, together with the masters of Industry, in its future development. Ours is the leadership of Education, advise us and help us, as to how we should best work out our views on the future of Education conformably with your views on the future of Industry." Stating this in the terms of the practical organizer—and I offer it for the consideration of the Rev. Simeon Flux— this is the sort of thing to be done. When, as it shortly will, University Extension shall have a few years record to show of its administration of County Council grants in different parts, for the direct application of Education to Industry, a circular might be drawn up, and sent round to all the Trade Societies, inviting their assistance for the furtherance of Education among workmen, according to the different Industries in which they were engaged, and inviting their co-operation on some such representative body as it might be deemed well to construct, for the purpose of giving the assistance reality. Here, then, we should have a sort of Federal Council of Trade Union Leaders, interested in Education as it bore upon their separate trades, looking to the Universities as their allies and leaders in educational matters, and pledged on their side to assist the Universities in furthering the Extension movement among working men. The influence that a council of this kind might exercise, in steadying or helping local committees, would be invaluable, and its indirect influence on the future educational policy of the County Councils is well worth considering. What we want is a machinery of some sort, that will make University Extension among workmen more possible, and now that University Extension is beginning to have a direct bearing on Industry, the method suggested would seem to be a first means to such an end.

At present, University Extension, among working men, as among other audiences, is greatly dependent on attractiveness. The local secretary, the district organiser, the incipient lecturer, are haunted with the bugbear of attractiveness. On all hands we hear, lecture smust be interesting or they 'will not pay.' Success depends on attractiveness. At the same time the Extension movement is accused of dilettantism. The one is the converse of the other. The nature of the movement necessitates this. When you are wooing you seek to please. Establishment will modify this. Nobody demands attractiveness of an academic lecturer, simply because he has a definite course, and the course once established the subject becomes more important than the man. We need not, I think, look upon the necessity for attractiveness as a permanent difficulty, it will settle itself; and inasmuch as we are dealing with a portion of the community, to whom, if University Extension is to mean anything at all, it will mean something definitely related to life, real, and not dilettante, we may regard this difficulty as not very serious in the future. But immediately it is a very great difficulty. University Extension courses are to attract the workman, and they often do not. This fact we should meet boldly; there is no blinking it: and we should meet it by giving the workman, not necessarily what is, but what appears to be, some immediate return for his money. We have done it with the elementary teachers, why should we not do it with the artizan? The recent recognition of the Extension certificate by the Education department has, and will more and more, set a premium on our educational system and methods of teaching; that is to say, the certificate has now a distinct bread-and-butter value to the elementary teacher. Without in the least wishing to encourage what one might call the bread-and-butter view of certificates in general,—Timothy Thumb's point of view, when he sent his sixty-seven certificates into the Board, and they elected him because he had the greatest number; I hold that we shall never fully win the workman to University Extension until we give the teaching a similiar bread-and-butter value to him. What we have done for the Elementary teacher we should also seek to do for the artizan. The problem is a much harder one, but it can be solved in one way only. University Extension must get direct at the machinery that controls production, just as it is getting direct at the machinery that controls Elementary education.

It will be long before this can be done in any way universally, but, accepting the policy, it would seem realizable by degrees. There is no reason, for instance, why we should not take different Industries separately, and one by one, and as it were, form cycles of study on them, grounded in the special and technical, and developing into the general and humanistic.

This suggestion I shall develop in the next chapter.

The workman and the elementary teacher in their joint relation to University Extension

There is no reason, if once we have acquired a firm hold on a particular Industry, why the Extension Certificate might not, in some cases, be a help to admission in that Industry, or be used as a complement to the training of apprentices, in the same way as, however inadequately, the South Kensington certificates have, in some cases been. Here is another thing for Messrs. Sky Sign and Co.'s school to do, had they but started it !

I do not wish it to be thought that I attach any value whatever to the certificate in itself. The Board elected Timothy Thumbs, but, as he expressively put it, "they did it by paper weight." The chairman of committee counted the certificates, and said ; " Gentlemen, I need not take up the time of Committee by reading all this literature. This man has got sixty-seven, the next only fifty-nine. I take it we should do well in appointing 'sixty-seven.'" So "sixty-seven" was appointed, and by a fluke, worthy of " Alice's Adventures in Wonderland," the best possible man got the post. " Fifty-nine," I never met. The inspired utterance of William Blake, when he described the Sons of Time as " striving with systems to deliver individuals from these systems," will hold good of the Extension system as well as of any other. Its present value lies in its spontaneity, and its power of " delivering individuals," but I regard it here as one amongst other means to an end, and that end is the humanizing of the artizan. Timothy Thumbs, at present, is all system and no deliverance ; Thomas Trudge is neither deliverance nor system.

But we have still to consider the wisdom of working through the elementary teacher with a view to touching the artizan. Timothy Thumbs is tied hand and foot in meshes of the Code, and we University men, who are perhaps too free ourselves, are unable to give him freedom. But there is one thing we can do for him, and there is one thing he, and he only, can do for us. He can hold the artizan of the future ; we, in recognizing him as our colleague in an educational movement amongst artizans, could guide him in the doing of this. Let me give an instance here, also, one among many of what might be done.

I have been often struck by the love and loyalty which Timothy Thumbs' Old Boys Club and University Extension the lad who leaves school at the age of fifteen, to enter some trade, shows for the teacher, who has wearily graded him through his standards (I need not say what devotion Timothy Thumbs' Old Boys' Club has for him). *There*, it seems to me, lies one of the forces of our movement. At present it is wasted for any definite constructive purpose. All our Education is valueless, and all our construction futile, unless we put it on a human basis. I should like to see these boys—the leaders of future labour movements, held already to their teacher by the most natural of all ties, held yet further, and not only held, but prepared and passed on by him to us. I should like to see what one might call "educational apprentices' unions," formed by elementary teachers interested in, and definitely connected with, University Extension. There will be no difficulty in doing this, only we must do it humanly, put a little of the human touch into the doing of it, and Timothy Thumbs can help us there before all others. In short, we must give to the teacher of the young artizan a definite place in the militant work of University Extension. If we did this, he would reveal to us a hundred ways of furthering Extension work among artizans.

These, then, are some of the main lines of the policy of University Extension among artizans, as regards method. There are many minor and indirect ways in which this policy can be furthered. Many ways in which our present methods could be extended to suit the special wants of working-men. I will not multiply instances, but such things as these suggest themselves—The development of the Summer Meeting, so as to make it even more attractive, and also more directly educational, than it is at present :—The development of the scholarship system in special trades, tenable for special purposes; and I would like to go further and see—but perhaps this is far to seek—certain scholarships held at certain colleges during the long vacation, thus giving the artizan a bond of connection—however slight it might be— with what is, after all, the body and soul of the English Universities, the collegiate system. Is it beyond the bounds of possibility to think that, given fresh endowments for these ends, the Colleges themselves might be induced to take the question up from their side? Possibly such speculations are premature, but let us always remember this, that the Universities, in extending their sphere of teaching into the great formless mass of British Industry, learn just as much as they teach—perhaps more!

I have now, however, superficially discussed some of the methods of the University Extension among working men. A few words are necessary in conclusion, since it is a policy

we are delineating, to guide those of us on whom fall the The quali-
responsibility of carrying out those methods in practice. fications
What are our marching orders? We lecturers, in so far pathies
as we have dealings with working men, and are prepared of the
to accept the policy sketched out above, have, as it were, to lecturer
express it personally. For this purpose, our first qualification,
other than the academic one, should be to have sympathy
in social questions : sympathy, distinctly non-political, and
such as will involve us in no industrial dispute, but sympathy
that is prepared to enter into equal relations, if need be,
with any party ; sympathy with Mr. Pushington, and the
responsibilities of Sky Sign & Co., when he takes the chair
at our inaugural lecture ; sympathy with Mr. Thomas Trudge,
when he heckles us after it is over, and asks us what is the
good of all this talk, unless we sweep clean the system.
The ideal to aim at seems to be a dual relationship, of a
human kind, between a liberally-minded central office on
the one hand, and the local centre on the other. *Freedom*
and *Personality*, in other words, are the two things of
importance, and in dealing with working-men centres, they
are of special importance. To promote these more effectu-
ally, every lecturer should, I think, devise means of continuing
his connection with any successful centre, after the delivery
of his course. There are many ways, especially through
Students' Unions, in which this could be done. It is
permanence that should be aimed at in these associations,
and ways and means might be devised, whereby the Students'
Union should be made to convene, as it were, councils of
its past lecturers, to guide its educational work. It would
probably mean little more than the cost of travelling expenses ;
for most lecturers would be willing to give occasional advice
to a centre that had done them credit.

As to the lecturer's further qualifications, little need be
pleaded for beyond the quality of sympathy, but in dealing
with working men, it cannot be too fully insisted that his
method of teaching should be elastic ; indeed, I would go
further, and say that it should be so elastic as to allow of his
substituting other methods of teaching, beside the lecture, if
he saw the need for so doing, and the Central Office should
help him in this. We should err, rather, on the side
of being *opportunist* than of being *doctrinaire*; and the not
ill-founded charge has already been made against some of
the Universities of demanding a too definite syllabus from
the lecturer, and of inflicting a too rigid course on the

H   105 centre. With working men particularly, it is much more the earnestness and personality of the man that teaches, than the previously defined curriculum which he is asked to lead them through, and it would seem wiser for the University to say "What is it you want, and we will see if we can give it you," than to say, "This is what you ought to want—so, Hobson's Choice, this or none!" But the point I would dwell on here is the responsibility that a lecturer himself should feel for the free hand granted him. His tact and his discretion, and the careful and loyal use, for the University for which he is working, of the freedom that is allowed him from a liberal-minded central office, are qualities which must in great measure depend upon the man himself, and cannot be forced upon him by any organization ; but he will have to recognize that it is the expression of his personality that is wanted of him before all other things, and that, for every result he achieves, and for whatever influence he exercises, through his personality, more and more responsibility will devolve upon him. This has been done, and this is his very doing ! The lecturer who is dealing with working men should, it seems to me, get to realize that he is responsible to his centre for what little fragment of learning he has to give, and to his University for how it shall be given. Both Mr. Pushington and the Rev. Simeon Flux are outside the real needs of his work. The lecturer is the lens on which the rays of light are gathered, and through him shall they be thrown upon the dark places of Industry.

CHAPTER 10.—THE POLICY DEVELOPED TOWARDS WORKSHOP RECONSTRUCTION.

But I want to lay down yet more fully what I challenged Mr. Pushington and the Rev. Simeon Flux to do—a policy in industrial Education, and I use the term as implying such portions of secondary and technical education as tend directly to the Improvement of Industry.

In our social problem of workshop re-construction, we have to consider the subject from many points of view, and also regard the possible bearing upon it of existing educational agencies, and of what national ideal we have in Education. If we take these various existing educational agencies, and ask how far they severally tend towards the direct improvement of Industry, we find that very few do so at all. The elementary schools, the basis of our national education, train the children of the " masses," and give the rudiments of general teaching. The Universities train the youth of the " classes," and, as the crown of this education, take their stand on a magnificent series of humanistic studies. Dependent on the Universities are the public schools ; and, partly dependent, mainly independent, are a variety of minor agencies, whose sphere of action is principally middle class, and whose curricula are partly humanistic, partly technical and commercial, often having special relation to sections of the community, but as ·yet doing little or nothing for purely industrial Education. If we ask for a policy from these different bodies, to guide us in considering the question of the future of Industry, they have none to offer.

They fall out, even as Mr. Pushington and the Rev. Simeon Flux fell out.

Now, there are three points of view from which the question of industrial education must be regarded, and these are, respectively, that of the producing body—the workshop or Industry, which implies the life of the workman, his mental and social development ; that of the endowing body —the County Council, or fund-collecting agency, whether central or local, and at present mainly controlled by the

The work-masters of Industry; and that of the highest educating
shop, the body—the Universities, whose militant attitude and rapid
County
Council transformation is bringing them face to face with the ques-
and the tion of industrial Education.
Univer-
sity In regarding the question from these three points of view,
we are brought into contact, respectively, with three difficulties:—first, the social problems of the workshop and the
force of Trade Unionism ; secondly, the question of middle-
class education, and the continuous diversion, towards this
end, of money and energy, intended at the outset for the
direct improvement of Industry ; thirdly, the question as to
how far any policy for industrial Education on the part of
the Universities might tend to impair that noble series of
humanistic studies which they have developed in unbroken
tradition from the Middle Ages, and in which all the great
statesmen and thinkers of England have been trained.

Any attempt at an answer, to these three problems, would
be outside the scope of this chapter, but each has to be
kept clearly in view when the question of a policy in industrial Education is being considered. I will endeavour here
to give, in greater detail, the outline of such a policy. For
want of anything better, it may guide us towards a clearer
understanding of the question of industrial Education, from
the three aspects just mentioned.

Three In doing so, however, it will be necessary to assume three
assump-things. First, that the workman, through his Union, will,
tions in the near future, as he is already now beginning to do,
take a definite line in his own interest, and insist on a
precise allocation of any moneys devoted to purposes of
education, and that, consequently, the Trade Unions may be
regarded as the governing forces of the future, in this respect.
Secondly, that the moneys recently placed in the hands of
the County Councils,—and these moneys are, at present, the
only definitely available for purposes of industrial Education
that we need here consider—will continue, and thus afford
a permanent means for developing our policy of industrial
Education. And thirdly, that the Universities will, in the
near future, either definitely leave alone, or definitely take
up, the question of industrial Education ; that they will
either say, " Our object is humanistic only ; we now draw
a circle around us, thus far do we go, and no further;"
or, " We maintain that our primary object is the humanistic
studies, but we are prepared, provided our action does not
militate against these, to come forward and assist in guiding.

this new National want, and, in meeting it, as we have met
the want for Science, the want for the higher education of
women, and the other great educational wants of the last
three decades." With this, I will also assume that, by
their recent action in administering for the County Councils
much of the moneys to be devoted for Industrial Education,
they are at present tending towards the second of these two
alternatives. On these three assumptions, how shall we
construct our policy ?

If we take any representative industrial centre, not Existing
necessarily a large town, what do we find ? A collection of and con-
small, and often inefficient, local organisations without any conditions
relation to each other. There is the Science and Art in indus-
Department, with its grant earning machinery ; there is trial
the University Extension Committee, dependent for the Education
most part on the popularity of its lectures and the energy
of its honorary secretary ; there may be varieties and
selections of technical or home arts' classes, dependent on
the personal influence of a paid or unpaid teacher, and there
is the new and tentative machinery for dispensing the
County Council grant—either through a well-intentioned, but
ill-informed, technical education sub-committee, or preferably
through a specially appointed organising secretary. These
are the only bodies through whom any attempt is made to
do anything for industrial Education.

Now, the action of all these bodies is at present divided,
broken up, often overlapping, and consequently wasteful ;
but not only this, it takes little count of where the force of
the future is to lie, and the consequent direction into which
its energy for the present should flow. The University
Extension movement, though constantly trying, is, owing
mainly to want of funds, hardly ever succeeding in its effort
to touch immediately the producers of Industry ; the Trade
Unions, and societies of workmen—the force of the future—
stand outside the educational question, and those, in whose
hands lies the dispensation of the funds for industrial
Education are, for the most part, half-hearted, and, by the
nature of their composition as masters of Industry, out of Univer-
sympathy with workmen's organizations. sity,Trade
Notwithstanding these obstacles, the only prospect of a County
possible working policy, under existing conditions, is to Council
make a union between these three factors—viz., the Universi- must work
ties, the Workmen's Societies, and the County Councils ; to mon
find some way by which they can work together to a common purpose

109

purpose. The Universities are the only bodies in the country that have both educational prestige and vitality; the body or bodies in whose hands lies the future of Industry, are the Trade Unions and workmen's organizations; the bodies with whom at present rest the funds, are the County and Town Councils. What should be aimed at is a co-ordination of these three, or at least a union on definite lines of the first and the third, with due regard to the potential action of the second. In other words, the Universities have the power of inception and direction; the Unions are the future, the County Councils the present, agents, by which any definite system of industrial Education would seem to be possible.

In the last chapter I urged the advisability of the formation by the Universities of some sort of Federal Council of representatives from the various Trade Societies to advise upon and assist in the question of Industrial Education in its immediate bearing on the artizan; such Council to stand at the side of the Universities in their dealings, however remote, with any particular Industry, and to watch the local action of the grant-giving committee in the interests of the artizan through his trade representatives. The suggestion was made rather in the belief that, if the Universities did not take the initiative in a matter of this kind, the Trade Societies would do it themselves, that this would mean conflict, and that harmonious action would be both more beneficial and more dignified for either party.

We can, however, leave out of consideration, for the present, the question of the action of such a Federal Council. Suffice it, that, in the future, it would be the strongest, perhaps the only, force necessary to guide the right alloca-tion of funds to be devoted to industrial Education. Concurrently, with the formation of such a body, then, what should the action of the Universities be, in relation to the local grant-giving agencies, in order that we may further develop the policy thus far sketched out?

Let me say at the outset, that I do not think the Univer-sities should in any way be pledged to *give* industrial Education themselves, but that their action, where called upon, should be to *guide the giving*, and that they should, from the point of view of education, as a whole, determine, to all education given, its definite place.

Some method of this kind should be adopted. Where there is a definite Industry or group of Industries, and a local agency empowered to grant moneys for its educational The cycle of Indus-trial study development, the Universities, in conjunction with, and at the advice of, the local authorities (it matters little for our purpose which takes the initiative), should draw up a scheme or cycle of studies, say of five or six years' duration, directly bearing on that Industry, not in any way *teaching the trade*, according to the legal interpretation of the term, but based on the technical, and passing through the scientific or artistic, into the humanistic studies, with which that, as every Industry, should be crowned. The examining and directive force should then remain with the Universities, the determining and variation of wants being left entirely to local expression. The method would act somewhat in this way. Supposing the Industry in question be any of the five following: pottery, mining, furniture-making, metal work (founding, brazing, casting, &c.), or ship-building; suppose also that the group of studies in the cycle be ranged under the six following heads :—

    (1) Social.
    (2) Historical.
    (3) Literary.
    (4) Artistic   { (a) Practical.
                  { (b) Theoretical.
    (5) Technical { (a) Practical.
                  { (b) Theoretical.
    (6) Scientific.

Striking out whichever one or two of these six was, at the outset, not needed by the Industry in question, the Universities should say "we can send you teachers for (1), (2), (3) and (6); for (4) and (5) we may, or may not, be able to accomodate you for the theoretical side, but we are ready, from the point of view of education as a whole, to draw up a cycle for and with you, to determine for and with you the relative value of the various studies, and to adjudge the respective application of the practical to the humanistic : also to send you someone of standing and position who may give educational order and method to the whole sequence." On the next page I give a suggestion of some such sequence, or cycle of studies, embracing the practical, and crowned by the humanistic, and such as might be applicable to some centre of metal—work Industry, or the production of metal—work, from the raw material to the completed article. It must be regarded as quite general, and not as having definite application to any existing Industry.

A SUGGESTED CYCLE OF STUDIES FOR A CENTRAL COURSE

I. SOCIAL.		II. HISTORICAL.		III. LITERARY.	
POLITICAL AND SOCIAL ECONOMY.		ENGLISH HISTORY.	FOREIGN HISTORY.	GENERAL LITERA- TURE.	SPECIAL LITERA- TURE.
The study of the position of the work- man.	The study of the development of the Metal In- dustries in England and abroad, illus- trated by the particular In- dustries here practised. e.g.: *The de- velopment of French or Ger- man metal work in its relation to the English market.*	Especially as illustra- ted by its bearings on the differ- ent periods of English metal work from the twelfth to the nine- teenth cen- turies.	Either as (1) bearing on the English periods or as (2) illus- trating the action of simi- lar Industries elsewhere. e.g.:(1) *The Re- naissance period and the influence of Italian design on the metal- workers of Fran- çois I. in France, or the metal- workers of Nur- emberg.* (2) *Greek jewel- lery and coins.*	To be re- garded as purely hu- manistic, and taken as being led up to by each special study. *This might be divided into—* (a) *English Classics.* (b) *Light reading.*	Works deal- ing with, or bearing on, the Indus- tries (but not of a Technical nature. e.g.: *Such books as the Auto- biograpy of Benuvento Cellini.*

N.B.—In connection with the above the following points have to be held in view :—

1. The whole scheme must be taken as a cycle of studies subsidiary courses, running through the whole period ;
2. The scheme to be under the guidance of one mind, the whole scheme.
3. The bench work, or purely practical, to be taken with,
4. The whole scheme to be so arranged as to meet the Teacher.

112

OF LECTURES.

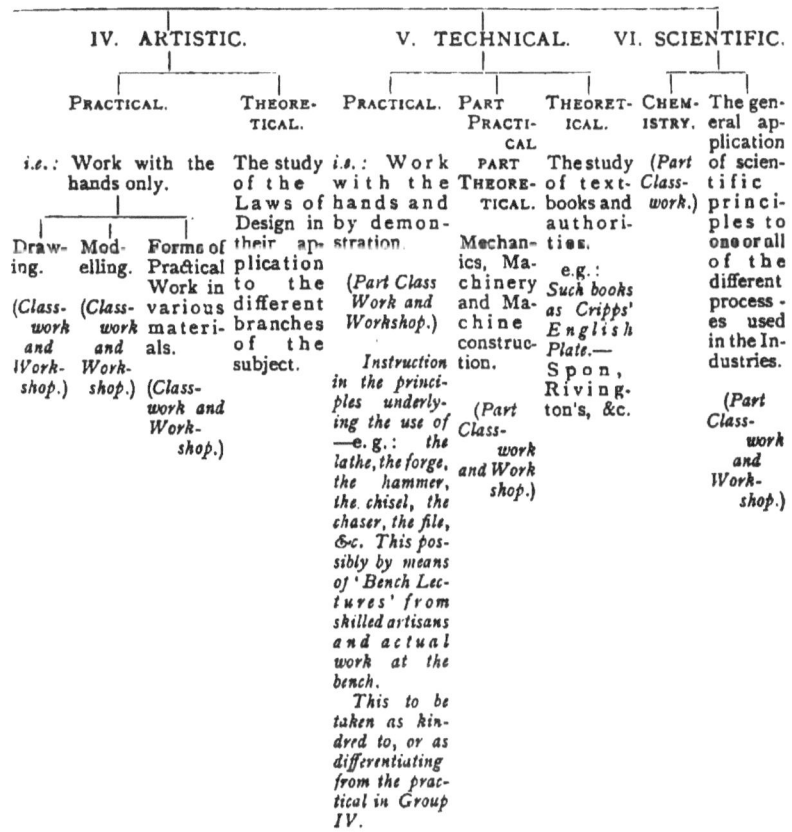

IV. ARTISTIC.			V. TECHNICAL.			VI. SCIENTIFIC.	
PRACTICAL.		THEORE- TICAL.	PRACTICAL.	PART PRACTI- CAL	THEORET- ICAL.	CHEM- ISTRY.	The gen- eral ap- plication
i.e.: Work with the hands only.		The study of the Laws of Design in their ap- plication to the various different branches of the subject. *(Class- work and Work- shop.)*	*i.e.:* Work with the hands and by demon- stration. *(Part Class Work and Workshop.)* *Instruction in the princi- ples underly- ing the use of* —e. g.: *the lathe, the forge, the hammer, the chisel, the chaser, the file, &c. This pos- sibly by means of 'Bench Lec- tures' from skilled artisans and actual work at the bench.* *This to be taken as kin- dred to, or as differentiating from the prac- tical in Group IV.*	PART PART THEORE- TICAL. *(Part Class- work and Work shop.)*	The study of text- books and authori- ties. *e.g.:* *Such books as Cripps' English Plate.—* S p o n , Rivin g- ton's, &c.	*(Part Class- work.)*	of scien- tific princi- ples to one or all of the different process - es used in the In- dustries. *(Part Class- work and Work- shop.)*
Draw- ing. *(Class- work and Work- shop.)*	Mod- elling. *(Class- work and Work- shop.)*	Forms of Pra&ical Work in		Mechan- ics, Ma- chinery and Ma- chine construc- tion.			

and arranged over a period of five or six years; a central course of lectures, with some higher certificate possibly being granted at the close of the cycle.

lecturers and practical teachers having their respective functions in reference to the

and as directly relating to, the whole scheme.

various requirements of (1) the Artizan; (2) the Apprentice; (3) the Elementary

Mr. Push-
ington's
curious
aloofness
The lecture, which in my last chapter I mentioned as being condemned by Mr. Pushington and the Rev. Simeon Flux, was the first of a series intended to lead up to a cycle of this kind, and, as far as they went, I consider them to have been successful. They have also led to others of a similar nature in other parts of England : lectures among metal-workers, chair makers, potters, furniture makers ; in every case the attempt has been to show the connection of Education with Industry, *to graft the humanistic on to the industrial*. The work has, of course, been very scrappy and slight, for the Extension system, as at present developed, admits of little else, but it has, as far as I can see, supplied a want, and, as an experiment, I think has justified its inception. Mr. Pushington's prognostics I do not hold to have been borne out, nor the Rev. Simeon's optimism either. Such lectures are, perhaps, a first move towards a new policy. Mr. Pushington has written very kindly, but somewhat epigramatically, to me on the matter.

"I am glad of your success, it is always gratifying to think one may be of some use. I think the fellows, of whom you write, are indebted to you for the time and trouble you have spent upon them. Possibly you may have a greater belief than I have in the cohesion of Oxford, Cambridge, and London, to one definite educational policy on the lines you lay down ; but before counting my Extension chickens, I should see them hatched at the three Central Offices, if I were you !

"Believe me,

"Yours faithfully,

"ARCHIBALD PUSHINGTON."

Academic
compro-
mising
I do not know whether I quite understand this letter ; others may possibly see its drift. Here, however, is the policy I propose, of the grafting of University Extension on to the Workshop—of the humanistic studies on to Industry. If we are really to confine ourselves to the *litteræ humaniores*, and that were a perfectly sound and logical position for the Universities to take up, let us adapt our present Extension curricula to that end, let us strike out the bulk of the Science Courses, and the Greek Art, and the Sculpture, and the Architecture, instead of compromising with the former, and playing, as we at present do, with the latter. Modern scientific courses are mainly asked for by Extension Centres, on the plea of a possible aid for the Industries of the district,

114

and chemistry as applied to leather tanning and mining can find no place in *litteræ humaniores*. As for courses on Greek sculpture, on architecture, on design, they have, as often now delivered, no relation to any existing Art, Craft, or Industry, and in so far, or unless taken on the questionable ground of the training of taste, may be said to be frivolous and irrelevant. They should be either accepted as parts of literary and historical courses, or unreservedly struck out.

Speaking as an architect, I hold very strongly, that courses on these subjects should only be given by artists and architects, though I should welcome a critical study of Greek statues and Gothic churches in the historian or the man of letters. However, all three Universities have compromised so far, and will probably continue to do so yet further.*

What is now not unreasonably asked in many quarters; The need for unre-served co-operation by the outside public; by the centres in many parts, whether under Oxford, Cambridge, or London jurisdiction; by a large proportion of the lecturers, who alone are cognizant of the details of the work outside the region of the three central offices, is, that the Universities should at last fix a common standard, abandon the uneconomic and wasteful system of "preserves," in centres, and "protection" in lecturers, and that they should work together for *Education* rather than separately for *Extension*, and in their relation to industrial requirements—either boldly go forward or firmly hold back. We have had wavering enough.

The policy I have sketched out above professes to be no Benefits from the policy more than a sketch from my own limited point of view, but if it is fully developed, and consistently applied by the Universities, working together in harmony, it would, I believe, carry with it the greatest possible benefits. Above all, it would secure three lasting advantages to the three agencies with whom it is mainly concerned. To the University Extension movement it would give further life, vigour, and reality, and by grafting it definitely on to Industry, would give it a much more genuinely educational character

---

* When one comes to examine the matter closely, it is clear that, granted a settlement on the disputed point of the six or twelve lecture course, there is really very little to choose between the positions they respectively profess to take up. They are agreed that it is the *litteræ humaniores* that should be primarily aimed at. Oxford frankly admits that it is using means to ends; Cambridge and London profess to hold out, but do not really, partly because their hands are forced by the greater success of Oxford, partly because their curriculum is quite as illogical, and quite as much one of compromise as that of Oxford; and, with whatever casuistry it may be explained, the three lecture course allowed, only under another name, by London, is a much greater concession to popular taste than the six lecture course allowed by Oxford.

than it can claim to have at present, owing to its somewhat precarious establishment on the leisure of the middle-class. To the local grant-giving agencies, the County Councils and so forth—it would give the sense that there was a strong and dignified educational authority to which they could constantly look to save them from the policy of Little Peddlington, by which so much money is continually being frittered away ; to the trade societies it would give a new and direct interest in the greater and constructive sides of the Industries in which they severally were interested, especially those Trade Societies that have won their laurels in the industrial wars of the century, and will soon no longer be militant, but have to face the harder problems of constructive organisation in Industry.

Here, then, is the policy, but its inception is only possible from one quarter. The Trade Societies are not yet ready to act, either cohesively or constructively, the County Councils and local grant-giving agencies are, by the nature of their being, precluded from other than local action ; the Universities alone are in the position to act and take the lead. The question is, will they do it ? I cannot help thinking that Mr. Pushington's metaphor is much to the point.

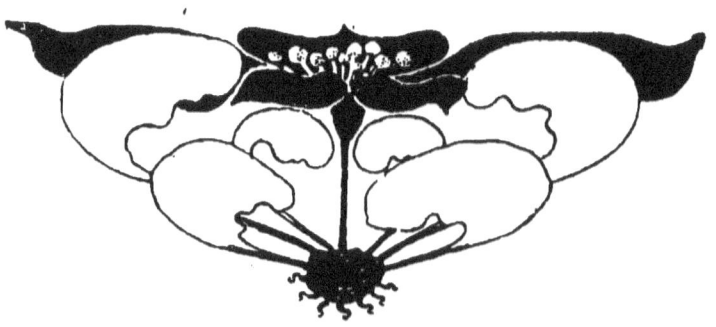

CHAPTER ii. — THE RE-LATION OF THE ARCHI-TECT TOWARDS WORK-SHOP RE-CONSTRUCTION.

AN ADDRESS TO THE
ARCHITECTURAL ASSO-
CIATION, 1892.

I purpose now to take up the subject of Workshop Re-construction from another point of view, the more special point of view of all those who are engaged in the building trades. How is the subject to be set before them, what is to be their line of action towards a sweeter and more genuine condition of things in the newer citizenship, and what is to be the relation, first of all, of the architect or comprehensive designer, to the workman or producer.

On the threshold of my subject, I would say that this relation of the architect to the workman, the right under-standing of it, and its application to his work as an artist, seems to me to be the most important part of that larger subject often called *The Relation of Architecture to Life.* I suppose, to most of us, the relation of architecture to life, is a question fraught with meaning in more senses than the narrow one of our own bread-and-butter ; but I would challenge every man to put his own interpretation on the question, and to ask himself what it actually means to him in the everyday humdrum of things. How he feels it ; whether, in the multitude of great architectural work, whether, in the poverty of good building, whether, in the absence of style, whether, in the eclectism of choice, whether, in his dealings with clients, with builders, with workmen, or how ? How, as an English architect, and, as a private individual ?

For my part, I think, the relation of Architecture to life in modern times cannot but be regarded as of the slightest. To *our* life, as architects, it means much, and always will ; to our life, as a nation, it means little—unfortunately for us. As a nation, we have small sympathy for, and scarce any

The relation of Architecture to modern life

understanding of, Architecture, and what sympathy and understanding there is, is limited to a few in the profession and their supporters. As a nation, we love show and vulgarity, with its concomitant cheapness; we love poverty of construction and its symbol, the iron girder; we love hurry and its resultant, the ill-considered moulding. We have not the great sympathy which could build the cathedral and forget the name of the architect; or the great power of reserve that could leave, in the consciousness of their harmonious development, the hundred details of the building to the craftsman. Architecture is no longer democratic, no longer understood of the people : it has lost its corporate significance. As a nation, we do not love Architecture; we are content to let our mouldings be struck with compasses, and our subtlest details be evolved by the office-youth; and we firmly believe that, when the assessor of the Royal Institute of British Architects has told us, or our representatives, the local committee, that this set of plans is the best we can possibly expect for the money, that it is good architecture we have got, and we thereupon proceed to what is called " merge the premium in the percentage."

I was comparing, lately, the conditions of some recent modern competition clauses, and the ethical frame of the English mind which these portrayed, with the document issued by the Florentines for the rebuilding of their cathedral in the year 1294. The British parallel, as it is familiar to most of you, I shall not give; the Florentine being less so, I will give you a portion of. Here is the key-note of it :—

And to mediæval life

" Since the highest mark of prudence in a people of noble origin is to proceed in the management of their affairs so that their magnanimity and wisdom may be evinced in their outward acts, we order Arnolfo, Head Master of our Commune, to make a design for the renovation of Santa Reparata, in a style of magnificence which neither the industry nor the power of man can surpass, that it may harmonise with the opinion of many wise persons in this city and state, who think that this Commune should not engage in any enterprise, unless its intention be to make the result correspond with that noblest sort of heart which is composed of the united will of many citizens."

It was this " united will," this " noblest sort of heart," which those old burghers felt could only be expressed by Architecture,—the mother Art. It seems somewhat of a mockery to speak of Architecture as actually being the mother

118

Art nowadays. Look at the walls of the Royal Academy at this moment—is it true? Look at Gower Street—is it true? Look at Greater London, "the desert of London town, grey miles long, the desert of London town, mirk miles broad," —is it true? Look at the public house, the restaurant, the nonconformist chapel, the average shop, the surburban villa, the Board school, the railway junction, the pit village, the factory town, and ask again,—is it true? When that phrase was invented, Building and Architecture were synonymous terms, we draw a subtle distinction, and say with truth, Yea, those be buildings: what we wish to deal with is Architecture,—the art of the Chief Builder, αρχι τεχτων, the essence of building. Possibly what we say is true in a double sense, but the truth is a bitter one.

Now, I do not say these things as a tirade against existing conditions. Tirades are futile and unnecessary for us as practical men, but I say them in order to point at ways that, by the energy mainly of the young architect, may be bettered, and at facts existing in modern life which, if rightly understood by him, will give him the opportunity of bettering them. To me it seems that this divorce of archi- tecture from the national life leaves its mark on him, and injuriously. He is not, if I may say so, and using the expression in the largest sense, sufficiently *educated*, not sufficiently—to put it in the famous term of the Italian Renaissance—*humanist*. His scope and sympathies, in the first place, are not wide enough, and then his technical training is not sufficiently all embracing; of this I shall have more to say in my next chapter. He finds that his "profession" or "art"—I use either word—is only becom- ing recognised as one of the polite arts or professions. It does not stand by the law, or the work of the doctor, or the school-master, or the many services of the State, or the University, in the public eye. Its position is doubtful, and it ministers in the main to the private comfort of wealthy men, not to the common heart of a great people.

As regards his method of work, he feels himself but a link in the productive chain. He sits in his office and makes designs, he has a connection, through specifications, with contractors, who carry them out, and he frequently anathematises a man of straw, who is known to him under the name of "The British Working-man," when they are not carried out properly. My contention is, therefore, that the architect, as yet, is not sufficiently educated in his

The Ar- chitect must be human- ized

relation to the "body social." It is, perhaps, unfair to say that he is (in a non-political sense) too conservative, but he has not that wide training in life which should make him sympathise with the greater movements of his time. His training is a narrow one, in the four walls of an office. He does not touch life directly, as the doctor or the clergyman ; he does not get glimpses into men and manners like the lawyer.

Here, then, we ask ourselves, If this be true, how can it be best remedied ? And we are brought face to face with the question of the relation of the architect and the work-man. The architect has to understand his position *as* a workman, in relation to other workmen ; more than this, he has to feel his responsibilities in organising and directing their work ; and more than that still, he should feel some direct responsibilities likewise, in training and educating them. Thus only will he deserve his title as architect or chief builder.

I will return to the consideration of this directly, in detail, staying for a moment to consider the question in its bearing on a matter very dear to all of us ; *style*, "the language of architecture." The architects of the late nineteenth century, have settled the question of style ; they have almost ceased to dogmatise ; the Battle of the Styles has been fought out, and a rough-and-ready compromise has been made between eclecticism and originality. That is style in its external sense ; but I believe we have also gone deeper : the inner question of the origin of style is what we are now solving. The origin of style lies not in the theories, not in the forms, of Art, but in the social relations of men to men, in their state of society, in their habitude to one another, in the leisure they may have for the thinking out of problems and the creation of forms. In short, the origin of style, is a social, not an artistic question. The question of style, therefore, is solving itself for the young architect, and will do so more and more as he grasps his relationship to the workman and the body social.

Style in Architecture fundamentally a social question

I repeat, then, that the young architect has to feel that he is a workman in a privileged position, in the position of giving other workmen their line of work. He is to be the "head master of our Commune ;" to fulfil this high function rightly, he must come into close and direct relation-ship with his fellows in every possible way.

Sir Charles Barry once suggested that it would be a good

thing for an architect with capital to invest it in building operations, and such work as might be in connection with architecture. That suggestion was a very wise and far-seeing one. Barry's age was, perhaps, not fully ready for it, but it has been, and is being, at the present day, acted upon by Architects in various ways. Regarding capital as the force that binds workmen together, regarding also the other great cohesive forces which were undiscernible to Barry,—the workmen's movements, &c., which are tending to a re-construction of Industry, at the present day ; regarding also the advisability, nay, necessity, of commencing (especially for the young architect) in the *ministering arts, the crafts* in other words, rather than in the mother art direct ; and regarding, in the last instance, the necessity of the frank recognition of the architect's connexion with Industry, Barry's sugges-tion, which implies the closer union of the architect to the body social, we might all set before us.

But I would give this suggestion more definiteness, and at the same time limit it. I would like to see applied to it the system of the old Craft Guild ; or such conditions as were possible of a society that produced the greatest Architecture of all time. In this society we find the right relation,—a more human relation between the architect and the workman.

Now, it seems to me, that there are three ways in which we are approximating to what was good in the old system. Three phases of modern development, which it behoves especially us younger men to study, and which all of them comprehend,—this better relation of architect and workman, upon which I would dwell in this chapter. These three things I might term " Craft-Guild potentialities," and they may be distinguished as follows : There is—

1. The existing connexion of architects with trade for artistic purposes.

2. The workmen's movements that are re-constructing Industry.

3. The educational movement—the humanism—that is making progress with rapid strides.

I will take them in order.

First of all, the existing connexion of architects with trade for artistic purposes,—the architect and the shop, let us call it. In the relation of the architect to tradesmen we see these Guild potentialities. We see it among the men employed by some of the leading architects,—his builders, his furniture makers, his painters, and so forth. I will put it plainer. In some cases the architect is in a position in which he can place his building with a particular builder with whom he has worked for years ; or if the contract is to be competed for, he can limit it to some three or four of those who have worked for him, and whom he can trust. In this, the Guild element enters. In some cases, an architect or group of architects, support a business in which stuffs, or furniture, or materials are produced specially from their designs, and to serve the purpose of their buildings. I use the word *support* advisedly, for, if their work is conscientiously done, more money of theirs goes into these businesses than ever comes out of them. Here, again, the Guild element enters. In some cases, again, the leading architects attract round them various small workmen—painters, carvers, sculptors, ironworkers— men of some special ability, whom they have met with in the course of their professional experience, and to whom they continue to give small jobs in one or other of their works. Here, above all, the Guild element enters, and with it an educational environment, and a constant and direct relationship between the employing architect and the producing craftsman.

Now, it seems to me, that we younger men have to take up this side of what one might call the professional tradition, and develop it. Here is a portion of our heritage that is worth having ; in this there lies a future.

We should get into closer touch with our masons, our carvers, our decorators. We should welcome, instead of glancing at them with the eye of false shame, the efforts of architects to work through the ordinary distributive agencies of the shop ; and, above all, we should unite to us a body of men—young men, if possible—who are capable of ministering to the various crafts dependent upon Architecture.

The step from this to the completed Craft Guild is a social one, and one that time must bring. The atoms at present are distributed, but the personality of the architect should unite them. Their interests, at present, are discordant—A loses what B gains ; the architect has it in his power to make them harmonious, by uniting them with him. Their training at present is incomplete, and each, if left to himself, would ruin the ensemble ; the architect, as having the grasp of the whole, has it in his power to teach, and so to give each his place, that left to himself he shall be trusted to understand his own limitation. I am a painter, and must feel the relation of these reds to the whole scheme of colour; I am a joiner, and must understand that this panelling must range with the architectural treatment of the frieze and cornice ; and so forth.

I should be as opposed as any man to the idea that the architect should be connected in any way with trade or with dealing, or should receive any remuneration other than that professionally established for professional services, or for purely artistic work of his own hands in connection with it ; but inasmuch as the architect's work is productive, so he should be in immediate touch with production : but I hold that an architect should have a workshop at his back, and come into constant relation with a body of men in various crafts educated with and by him.

Then we come to the next point,—the workmen's movements,—the great underlying questions of the development of Industry, its re-organisation, the evolution of Co-operation and co-operative societies,—and the workmen's insistence on the raising of the standard of life, a purely mediæval repetition in many respects. These things the young architect should study, and should learn to make use of, and not to shun. *The Architect and his relation to the workmen's movements*

The real interests of the day are, and probably will be for the next decade or so, social : not political, not artistic, not directly educational. I hold it the duty of the young architect, if he wishes to get more into touch with life, to learn to take an intelligent interest in these workmen's movements. The knowledge or interest of the architect in them at present is often limited to the "strike clause" in the contract. I know it is the opinion of many artists, professional men of standing, that the Art may take care of itself, that social questions and ethics have no place whatever in Art ; and they accept the teaching of what might be called the reaction,—an inevitable one,—to the doctrines of John Ruskin. They hold that all the architect should care about is the final work produced. Does it or does it not conform to his designs, — no matter how it has been produced ? This might be right enough for the landscape painter or the artistic antiquarian, but I hold it to be absolutely and fundamentally false for the architect. I insist that the architect is in the position of the highest producer, and so should he bear the responsibility of the highest production.

He should study it, get to see its bearing on his work and those that work under him; he should seek to unite them co-operatively as producers, and without middlemen between them and him. There is nothing so painfully instructive to one as reading the habitual tone of scornful unsympathy expressed by the leading building papers whenever a question relating to workmen's movements, strikes, and industrial struggles comes forward. These papers, presumably, express professional opinion, but they are unreservedly biassed in favour of the employer as against the employed. It is for the young architect to study better these relations of capital and labour. If he does, he will see that there is no real antagonism between capital and labour : that the apparent antagonism of the present day is, in the first instance, one of *degree in remuneration for services ;* in the second instance, of *degree in control* between master and men; and that, in the first of these two, is implied the regulation of the standard of life, and on this standard of life good work depends.

The Architect's duty towards industrial Education

Now, to my last factor in the modern movement, in which lie Guild potentialities—educational development. The old apprenticeship system is dying out. It still remains in a somewhat unsatisfactory condition in architecture, and in such crafts as book-binding, that have in them some of the old-world element undestroyed by the machine, where the hand still holds, and which have not yet quite sunk into the slough of industrial despond; but, for the most part it is finished. Side by side with it we see a new growth—the technical school, which is even offering to take its place.

But the technical school never has taken and never can take its place. The technical school can only be a continuation, it can never supersede the workshop, it can never, as far as we can at present see, teach the actual trade itself as an apprentice should learn it; and certainly, according to the Technical Education Act, it may not even profess to teach it.

Edward Bellamy, in his *Looking Backward*, made the trenchant statement that, in the new state, a new force must take the place of the " master's eye " of the old trade system. This new force was " the perfectness of the organisation." I would accept this entirely, insisting only that perfectness of organization comprises " humanism."

Now, with the apprenticeship system dying, with the technical schools admittedly not fulfilling the required

124

conditions, and with the organisation of Industry imperfect, what is the educational outlook, as far as the architect is concerned? We have, it seems to me, to recognise that the apprenticeship system, regarded educationally, has been destroyed by subdivision of labour, and it is this subdivision of labour that we architects have to grapple with, it is here, that, by virtue of our position, we can be of service. We must help in the educational side of that reorganisation of Industry that is taking its place, not only in our own immediate art, but in all the handicrafts subordinate.

I would urge you all to consider how far it is not within the scope of the profession, by entering more into the study of the crafts, by approaching more the men in their movements, by working more in workshops and less in offices, to supply somewhat that which is wanted educationally, to enter into this educational movement, in its humanist and its technical side, which we see going on on all hands.

I have now indicated the three main lines in which it would seem to me that in dealing with the question of the relation of the architect to the workman, we younger men, having in mind the greater and more comprehensive development of the profession, have to look,—its development, in fact, more in conformity with the ways and methods of the mediæval Guild. Let me now sum up the position of the architect as I conceive it should be, in his relation to the workman,—an architect's ideal, if I may be allowed the term.

We should, in the first place, then, regard ourselves more as workmen, on whom fall the duties of production and of organization, and less as gentlemen of the office. As far as our own training goes, we should draw as little as possible, except from the human figure, but, with our hands, work as much as possible ; or, rather, I should say, we should seek to express our detail designs as much as possible *in actual material*, and not on paper—that is to say, in the workshop. Working thus in the workshop, we should grow into the sympathies of the workshop, and then seek to develop our position as organizers and employers of Industry. We should train up a body of men with us ; it is only by educating workmen in architectural principles, and ourselves in the relation of the handicrafts to our work, that style—real living style— not the shell of it in a modern Gothic church, or Queen Anne mansion—can come. At present, we act as a disintegrating force, and tend to keep the craftsmen asunder. We have sense enough to see that we can get better work from them, when they act as units, than when they are under the control of a contractor, or a big firm. It should be our effort to secure the advantages of freedom and spontaneity in work which a Guild system would give, without losing those advantages of business method and order, which the present system ensures. We ought, in fact, not to use a good craftsman as an artistic convenience, as we are tempted to do at present; but we should hold him, bind him to us,—as it were, take him into partnership with us,—and so take more responsibility for the *man*, and less responsibility for the *work*. By so doing, we should avoid that waste which, at the present day, always tends to convert the good craftsman into the bad employer of labour. The architect, more than any other person, has the blame of this; the architect, more than any other, ought to strive to prevent it. In the two following chapters I shall go into these hard sayings more fully, meantime I would ask the younger architect turn over in his mind some of Mr. Trudge's ideas on the collectivist re-organization of Industry.

CHAPTER 12—ON THE POSSIBILITY OF A METROPOLITAN SCHOOL OF ARCHITECTURE.

In the formulating of our municipal wants, somebody has suggested that we shall have a Metropolitan School of Architecture.

The artist, and the educationalist, alike, welcome such an idea, but there are many more things implied in it than at first sight appear. We are, all of us, agreed, I suppose, that such a school should give us a better chance for the training of our young men, should help us in the understanding of what beautiful Architecture of the past we yet possess, and should make possible the creation of fresh work in touch and sympathy with newer wants, and bearing the impress of the younger ideas; we are not, all of us, agreed, as to how far such a school shall help teach towards the solution of the social problems to which Architecture is tied, how far it shall help the reconstruction of the workshop, how far it shall be conducted on antiquarian lines, how far it shall be state-aided, and how far it shall be comprehensive in its inclusion of the representatives of the building trades generally. Few of us, I should say, have a sufficient grasp of the conditions of the profession of Architecture, and the building and affiliated trades, to take a wide enough survey of the subject from which to generalize, and still fewer are able to offer any definite constructive policy for the carrying out of our plan—at present a dream. We would like to see in London that spirit which inspired the Florentines when they ordered Arnolfo to rebuild the Cathedral, but, for the nonce, we have to take the cold comfort of the County Council, and the biting criticisms of the building papers on its good intentions.

Before we pass to the consideration of how we could construct this school of ours, let us take stock of what we have, in the way of existing Educational machinery, that professes to do something for architectural teaching.

There are the Royal Academy Schools, there is the Royal Institute of British Architects, with its examination system, there is the Architectural Association, with its meetings and

its curriculum for training, there are the newly created
Polytechnics, with their fragmentary classes, and there are
the private offices of architects, with teaching based on the
apprenticeship system. That is all; now what does this
represent ?

The Royal I put the Academy first, out of compliment to the Academy,
Academy compliments are customary with the Academy, and it likes to
and its have compliments paid it. But, I fear, as far as Architecture
Compli-
ments goes, compliments are all that it can either give or receive.
Dead, dead, and apparently past all hope of resurrection,
are the Academy schools, in their relation to architecture !
The bestowal of those glittering letters upon an occasion-
ally eminent architect, whose career and study have been
formed entirely outside it, the delivery of a few lectures,
often drearily antiquarian, in its splendid rooms, the offer
of a few prizes, and the annual yearly exhibition of architectural daughtsmanship, many of the drawings being by
the same hand, and that not the hand of the architect, is,
I believe, all that the Academy would itself claim to do for
English Architecture. To suggest to a pupil of any of the
leading architects, academicians, for instance, that he
should look to the Academy for his main source of teaching,
would be received with a laugh of derision.

The Royal Next comes the Royal Institute of British Architects,
Institute, more letters, but not more learning. The Institute has an
its letters,
and its ex- Examination, and grants Certificates, but I back Timothy
amination Thumbs, the Elementary Teacher, who has specialized on
examinations and certificates, to earn the Institute's letters
after a year's reading, and come out with honours, before
any living architect. But Timothy Thumbs, though I love
him dearly in his own school, and over a glass of whiskey,
I know to be a man of no constructive ability, and little
imagination, and having nothing to gain by tacking A.R.I.B.A.
on to his other Degrees, he wisely leaves them alone. The
Local Board of Great Fadwell East will not give him the
next evening continuation school job any the sooner.

It may almost be stated as a law in educational economics,
that an examination system, given a few generations and
an average ability to work on, will produce any standard
desired, up to a certain point. Its limitedness, its definiteness, and its rigidity make this possible. But then let us
not be deceived by it, we may gain in caligraphy, but we

128

lose in character, develope verbiage, but forget care; and there are certain qualities to which no examination test can possibly be applied, to wit, *the sense of Beauty, constructional ability, and human sympathy*: these are the architect's three fundamental needs, not knowledge of strains and styles.

It is a sufficient condemnation of the Institute's test, to point to the fact, that all the office boys, and assistants, and country draughtsmen, who are not likely ever to leave their mark on architecture, are eager to be tried by it, while almost all the artists, to whom we look for the future of English building, condemn it. How far behind the times, too, the Institute is, may be noted from the fact, that while the Universities and our leading Educationalists are beginning to abandon, or, at least, modify, the examination test, even in subjects where examination can be applied, the Institute is seeking to impose it even in subjects where the test is impossible. In addition to its examination, the Institute also has a valuable library, and rules for the guidance of professional practice, so, it is to be hoped, have Tom, Dick, and Harry; but their rules are of little help to you and me, who are so unsympathetic and independent, and Tom, Dick and Harry do not lend us their books—why should they?

˙Mr. Pushington once put me a very pertinent question— Mr. Push-
" How is it that you, who are such an advocate of Trade ington's
Unions in Industry, should be up in arms against anything ary perti-
approaching to a Trade Union in your own line; and how is nence
it that most members of the Institute, which is one of
the leading Trade Unions in the country, should be so
uniformly averse to Trade Unionism?"

It took me a very long time to think out the answer to this question, and, finally, I found it best to state my answer thus: " I am willing," I said, " to accept the Trade Union principles, provided there is a due recognition for artistic individuality. I do not, however, consider it in accordance with Trade Union principles, that the men of one trade should make laws for another. The members of the Royal Institute, estimable gentlemen, all of them, and composing one of the most dignified and important Trade Unions in the country, do not deal with architecture purely—architecture as an Art—but take under their supervision many other things which appear to them as, if not more, important. I do not, therefore, think that they should make laws for the artist, and they should certainly not apply an examination which cannot possibly test creative ability." As for the second part of the question, why is the Trade Union of the Institute so out of sympathy with the other Trade Unions of the country—the Workmen's Unions? I framed my answer thus: "Because the existence of 'professionalism' in Architecture is dependent on the life of the contracting system, and the contractor; it is against this system that the Trade Unions are striving, but which is upheld by professionalism and Architecture as a profession."

The Architectural Association and its educational endeavours. In the Architectural Association, we have young blood; we also have the invaluable element of combination, the Trade Union element, without the professional intimidation and picketting. In the Association's Union, we are allowed to be blacklegs, and an artist dearly loves being a blackleg. The question is, what does it do for Architectural Education? For it is the only body that is making any conscientious endeavour. I think, in its way, it does a good deal, but it is timid, its councils appear divided, and it does not seem quite strong enough, as yet, to stand alone. Given to the keener spirits of the Architectural Association, some closer study of the social problems that surround Architecture, in its contact with Industry, and we have one of the strongest factors for educational development and workshop re-construction in the metropolis. At present the Association's line is not clear.

The Polytechnics and their relation to Architecture Next come the Polytechnics and technical schools. I have sought above to give some expression to the big Polytechnic point of view, and its bearing on the teaching of Art.*

When Mr. Pushington, now some five years ago—in 1888 I think it was—founded the famous Upper Galore Polytechnic, I ventured to express my doubts to him as to the wisdom of the proceeding from the point of view of the constructive artist, and I have, since, had those doubts confirmed. The Polytechnics are not doing, and never can do, the work they are professing, or what has been hoped from them. No one denies for a moment that much of what they do is admirable, and much of it may be useful to the young architect, but it

* See page 27 to page 38.

is not what we imagine them to be doing, their action is supplementary only, they are not touching the workshop, and the workshop in the present instance is *the architect's office* and *the builder's yard.*

But what is the architect's office doing? Here, surely, with an apprenticeship system still in force, with the possibilities of personal contact between master and pupil, and with the apparent close relationship between the teaching function and the workshop function, as the youth is taught on his master's job, we may expect some training in Architecture; and indeed what teaching *is* done, we find in the office of the architect, but how limited, narrow, inefficient and unhuman it is. In the average architect's office the bulk of the work is clerical and draughtsmanship. The paid *assistant*, the *paying pupil*, and the *improver*, who comes to be " finished," but neither pays nor is paid, are set alike to the dreary and unprofitable work of inking in plans and making tracings. It matters not much if they understand, so long as the work is rapidly done, and the necessary sub-division of labour allots to one man the making of the "client's sketches," to another the plans, to a third the perspective views, while others again attend to the legal and surveyor's work, and the correspondence. They are all in the *profession.* Meantime the real building is being done outside the office, and by whom? Not the architect and his pupils, but the contractor and his men, and the real constructive teaching is not being given to the young men at all. No architect's pupil thinks of working with his own hands, doing a piece of carving, or bench work, and as to a little figure drawing—the boss does not do it, why should he? And, moreover, where should he? Imagine a nude model in the office of a City architect! What an amusing situation it suggests!

I was told by an eminent living architect, a pupil of the late Sir Gilbert Scott, that when, as an apprentice, he had completed his twenty-fourth perspective view, he struck, and timidly asked the master if he might learn something else. Now, judging from the rate at which the average articled pupil works,—and the articled pupil is not paid piece work,—he could not have taken less than two weeks over each perspective view, and thus a rough estimate may be arrived at as to what architectural training he acquired

The Architect's office and the apprenticeship system

during his three years' apprenticeship. The corollary of this is in a question that I once put to another of our eminent living architects, also a pupil of the late Sir Gilbert Scott, and the reply I got from him.

" How is the young architect to learn the practical details of building ? "

" Oh," was the answer, " he will get all that on his first job."

" And," I have since, in strict secrecy, added to myself, " at the expense of his first client."

The professional Architects and the Memorialists

All this is wrong ; yet none of our architects, least of all, the eminently practical ones, have any remedy to offer.

And their opponents, for instance the authors of that excellent book,* that made such a flutter in the professional dove-cots a few years ago, have no remedy for this either. The cry of the Memorialists is "leave us alone, and let us work at our Art as artists." My sympathies are entirely with the writers of this book, but I venture to think that they do not go far enough. Their point of view is invaluable as a critical one, but that is its limit ; and it is the point of view, not of the constructive artist looking to the future of his Art, but of the individual craftsman. Though it may not be within the province of any individual artist to consider the educational question in Art, it certainly behoves us, in our corporate action, to take into consideration the Architecture of the future, and until the Memorialists look at the whole question rather more comprehensively, and not only from the point of view of their own offices and studios, the enemy, that is to say, the *professional architect*, will remain in possession. To those of us, who wish to re-construct the workshop, their negative position differs only in degree from that of their opponents.

The prospects of architectural Education

How do we stand then ? With a Royal Academy that is contributing nothing to the educational welfare of our young men, with a Royal Institute, whose contribution is narrowed down by commercial considerations, and tacked to a system of examination which does more harm than good—with an association of younger architects, who are hesitating as to what lead to follow, and not apparently strong enough to take up a position of their own, with a variety of new technical schools, all unrelated, all fragmentary, and all

---

* " Architecture a Profession or an Art " (1892).

without guidance, or purpose, and with a system of office-teaching, in which the good old methods of apprenticeship are stultified by the sub-division of labour and the system of builders' contract, the need for mere draughtsmanship, and the intrusion of the work of lawyers, surveyors, and men of commerce into the workshop of the architect; where do we stand in the eyes of the official receiver of Ideas? Assets meagre, liabilities unmentionable, net result Educational Bankruptcy. The outlook for the education of our younger men is not a bright one—I hold it to be very serious indeed.

What then is to be done? Those of us, who are capable of taking a sufficiently large survey of the position we are in, realize how difficult is the problem; see well the educational embroglio, out of which we have to come clean, before we can hope for a sound system of teaching towards a School of Architecture in the largest sense of the term. But what are we to do? Work on existing lines? Found new institutions? It seems to me we must do both; but we must, first of all, look below the surface of things and discover what the real forces are underneath; the vital forces, I mean, those that, from the point of view of the Art and Craft of Architecture, hold the future in them.

These forces are two, and both curiously regarded with a certain amount of contempt in the Architectural profession. The *Artist Architect*, as he has been scornfully called, and *the Trades*, as represented by the Workmen's Unions. Both of these we have to tune to that note of reconstruction which I have sought to strike throughout in these essays. Our Metropolitan School must be formed on the basis of the reconstruction of the Workshop, and the Workshop, in this instance, includes the builder's yard and the architect's office. The forces of the future

The artist architect is the first of the forces we have to consider; and by the artist architect, I mean the architect who regards his subject as an Art, rather than as a Profession, who does not undertake surveying, and light and air jobs, who distinguishes between the work of the lawyer and the artist, following the latter; it is to him ultimately that the building of the century will be most indebted Our other force is the trades, or, more definitely, the different agencies for the The Artist Architect and the Trade Unions production of commodities for building, or the making of works of handicraft ; agencies whose real life we have to seek, not among the entrepreneurs and the holders of capital, but in the Unions and combinations of workmen who in each case produce for them.

The artist architect and the workman are the only two forces that we need be mindful of in the forming of our school. The employer of labour, entrepreneur, dealer in commodities, surveyor, lawyer, etc., we need not, for the present, take into consideration; if they come into our school, so much the better, we shall teach them some Architecture, but their special subjects will not be taught, except in subordination to the constructional and æthestic considerations of Architecture. For the architect, therefore, and for all those who are engaged in the constructive and decorative arts, the school shall be intended, and I would like to see Thomas Trudge there, and his son, and also my old friend, Mr. Pennyworth, the designer, but I doubt whether he would hold it worth his while, and for the present, moreover, he is under lock and key in the great safe of Messrs. Sky Sign and Co.

A sugges-
tion for a
practical
School of
Archi-
tecture

Paper schemes are unprofitable, but I will venture a sketch of how such a body as the Architectural Association, in which there is young blood, might actually construct for itself a Metropolitan School of Architecture. The idea will, doubtless, be considered unpractical, but then everything is unpractical until one or two earnest men are convinced of its practicability, and then it suddenly takes shape. A Metropolitan school in which, while the real teaching is being done, the re-construction of the workshop is taking place also.

Let there be, say a hundred young architects, nay fifty, even ten righteous could do it ; let them unite together to carry on, between them, a workshop, educational and productive, in which they and their pupils should learn, and in which their work should be carried out. When I asked a sculptor friend of mine the other day to give me his ideas as to how such a school should be formed, he said, "You must do two things first ; you must do away with the snobbish-ness of the architect, and you must train all your men, architects, sculptors, painters, together." Exactly. The architect must take off his top hat, and discontinue poking

134

at the workmen's clay model with his two foot rule when he makes his didactic visits to the contractor's shop. In this school he must set to work in an apron with the other workmen. My ten righteous should, in the first place, decide to make the teaching, in this school workshop, comprehensive, so as to include all who touched upon the building trades. To do this they should place in it, among the teachers, one or two practical workmen in touch with their Trade Unions.

These men should be put on a footing of equality with the architects, as far as the internal workshop government was concerned, and the workshop should be conducted on the lines of an industrial partnership, the workmen thus having a direct personal and corporate interest in the production of the work. The workshop being thus conducted on a co-operative basis, the capital and plant would, according to arrangement, belong to architect and workmen together, and, assuming a careful management, the economy effected by the elimination of the contractor and his profit, the saving of waste to the superfluous draughtsman—albeit the miserable man's wage is not a high one,—and the direct personal supervision of the architect, over the work produced, would make it possible for all the work to be turned out at a much lower rate than by the ordinary firm. Of the advantages to the art and craft of Architecture, it is needless to speak, for it stands to reason, that where the workman is interested, and where architect and workman alike, are in a position to leave the impress of their individuality on a piece of work, it must be better done. But I ask more still, my fifty righteous should not only pledge themselves to support this workshop, but also to let their pupils spend so many hours, or days, in each week to work in it, for, if we cannot destroy the professional office right away, we can, at least, impose limitations on ourselves towards humanizing it.

Established on a workshop and co-operative basis.

The advantages of such a workshop would be briefly these—architect and workman would be creating together. The younger men, and the older, too, if they cared, would have some chance for practical training; the workman himself, who was creating with and for the architect, would be trained and interested; the contractor and the contracting system would be at a discount; for, as the workshop grew and undertook co-operative contracts of its own, and

/   135

work of a larger kind, the old system would tend to disappear, for the prestige of such a guild-workshop for the profession could not fail to be considerable, and the work would be better and cheaper done. In short, we should be accomplishing two things, we should be doing what throughout these essays I have insisted on, viz., connecting the teaching function with the workshop function, and, in so doing, we should be directly applying the Guild system of the mediæval builders, *i.e.*, a co-operative and constructive one, to the modern profession and trades : be it added, to the great purification and service of both.

As to the details of how all this should be done, I do not intend here to speak ; details are not settled in essays, but have to be considered in relation to the individual men who are constructing, to their characters and personalities. But I will anticipate the taunt that the thing cannot be done, by the reply that the thing, on a small scale, already has been done, and its methods can be illustrated and tested in the now seven years' fairly successful work of the Guild and School of Handicraft. I venture to think that those of my architectural colleagues who regard it, in the long run, as an impossibility, do so because they are out of sympathy and, may I be pardoned for adding this, inexperienced in the great underlying social forces that are making for the reconstruction of Industry. Everything, I repeat, is unpractical, until one or two earnest men are convinced of its practicability, then it suddenly takes shape.

The doing of this, therefore, rests with the young men. They, who have much to gain and little to lose ; they, who are dissatisfied with the existing system, under which they work, and yet do not see where to turn for guidance, or what to do.

To the fifty righteous To the young men, I say, come out of it ! Leave the beaten track, and try the fresh way through the woods, if you lose yourselves awhile, it matters little, your time will not be misspent. Come away from Bloomsbury, and Holborn, and the City ; and start your offices in healthier places, near the workshops of the workmen, or where you can lead the freer life of the artist. You cannot do your work well under the old-fashioned conditions of the *professional office*. The inner room for the boss, and the outer room for the office boy. Have a place where you can work out

136

your own designs with your own hands, where you can have the living model to draw from; can set up a large cartoon if you need it, and can fashion a piece of clay for yourself, instead of poking at the workman's sketch with your two-foot rule, when you go on your didactic visits to the contractor's shop.

Our older architects are tied, hand and foot, to the contracting system, they cannot guide us, their sympathies are with the masters of Industry, they join in the hue and cry against the " British working man," and when they find their designs misunderstood, or their works stopped for a strike, lay the blame on an imaginary "agitator," and a Trade Union with which they are entirely unacquainted. This is an old-fashioned point of view, and to the young men, I say, drop it. Try and find out what the conditions are, under which the workman is doing your work, remember that he is at war with the contractor, with whom you are signing your agreement, try and discover what is really the reason of this war, and why it is so absorbing to him, and your work not at all absorbing; it is not a little or an unhelpful lesson that you will learn from this, and when you have answered, to your own satisfaction, one or two of these questions, and got into some little sympathy with the workman, see if you cannot then let him construct direct *for* and *with* you, without any middle man to whom he shall be responsible for his creative life. We architects are in a unique position, so far as labour is concerned, and this none of us appear to see. We are employers of labour, without taking the profits of labour. That, alone, is enough to make the workman trust us, and it is a duty we owe to our Art, as artists, to see that he does his work under the same pleasurable conditions as we do ours. In other words, I repeat what I said before, we must take more responsibility for the man, and less responsibility for the work; that is our duty, as younger men, who are seeking to establish a healthier order, and to be abreast with the times.

With such a spirit within us, we can set to creating our The fifty Metropolitan School of Architecture. Given fifty earnest righteous men holding these ideas, having sympathy for the labour movement, having tolerance for the narrowness or ignorance of the workman, and ready to break with the old condition of things in the profession; fifty earnest men, subscribing to, and supporting, a workshop of their own, in which they shall themselves study, in which their pupils shall study, into which they shall pledge themselves to place their work, and in which they shall all have a financial stake : given this, and our Metropolitan School of Architecture is already founded. We can snap our fingers at the County Council, and we need no benefaction from Mr. Pushington to help us. We can do it all ourselves, why should we not set about and do it ?

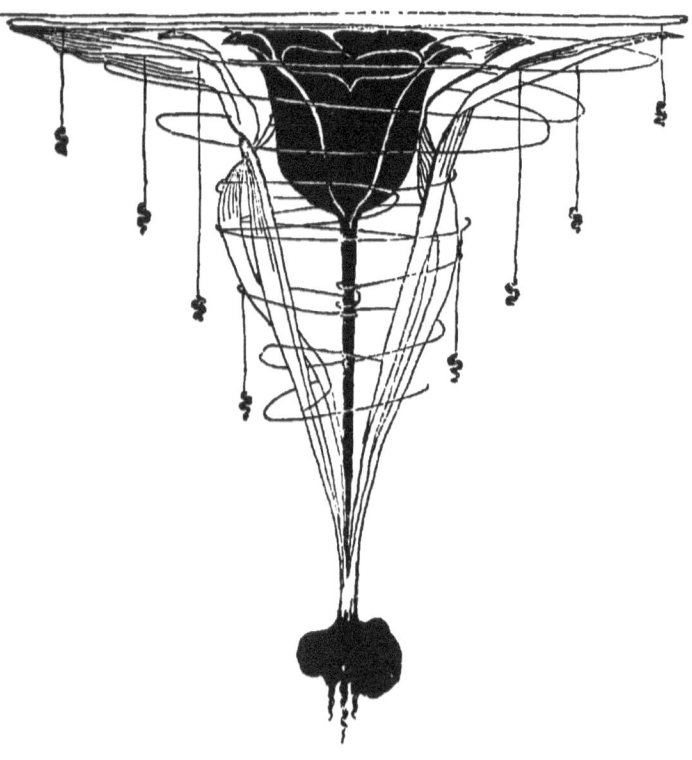

CHAPTER 13.—WHERE IS THE BUILDER OF IDEAS?

It might almost seem that, in attaching so much importance to the position of the architect, in my consideration of the re-construction of the workshop, I am forgetting that of the builder—who is, after all, the more important person of the two—I consecrate this chapter to him.

First of all, what is the builder? To anyone not in the secret of things, it might appear that the builder is one who builds, and that if the architect has, somehow, got into a false position, and become divorced from his material, the builder, at least, is much the same as he was, bar the artistic instinct, in the days, say of, John Thorpe, or William of Wykeham. Our problem of re-construction would be simple, indeed, if this were the case, for all we would have to do, would be to let our young architects be trained by, and work with, builders. The builder of to-day is nothing more nor less than a business man, who deals in a particular article, *i.e.*, the buying, selling, arranging, and general manipulation of materials for building—*how*, does not matter, as long as building Acts are conformed to, the very soul and life of his occupation ;—the how, the why, the purpose, of building, has gone out of his craft. Like the Cheapside tradesman, who does not make his goods himself, but has printed upon them " made by me," so the builder has the house built by a variety of different agencies, or men, whom he employs, and then paints upon the board above the hoarding, " Built by Thump and Co., builders and decorators." To put our work into his hands, from the point of view of the general public, would not be satisfactory, because it is not, primarily, in his interest to build, but to deal in building, and as this dealing in building is a most complex and difficult operation, and as complexity breeds complexity, the general public has recourse to the architect to check the builder, and see that his dealings are honest. All this is wasteful and superfluous, and is based upon a fundamental mistrust among the parties engaged — client, architect, builder, and workmen ; with some there is more mistrust than others, but everybody, by the nature of the system, mistrusts the builder. The professional contracting system, of which the builder is the centre and mainstay, amounts, therefore, to this : an architect, with little knowledge of the practical details of building, looking after a tradesman, whose interest is a purely commercial one, and who, in his turn, looks after a variety of partially trained workmen, who, owing to the nature of the position in which they are placed, have no interest in the work at all. As a system, it does not seek to produce good work, but, by a variety of ingenious checks and counter-checks, to prevent bad. I do not wish it to be thought that I consider good work cannot be done under this system, or that builders may not be honourable and conscientious men, but I insist that, where good work is produced, it is in spite of the system, and not because of it.

Now, I am on the look out for a Builder of Ideas, who will work with me to a newer end. I believe he exists, and that I shall find him. To this imaginary man I speak, as follows, and call to him out of the dark.

To the Builder of Ideas   You, my friend, are interested in social matters, and you have what, for want of a better word, I will call a con-science, I believe, far down, you also have the elements of an æsthetic sense, but that is not so important here, what is important is that you are a business man, and not ashamed, like most business men are, of admitting it. As you also have some sympathy with those who are seeking to recon-struct the Workshop, I want you to enter into a plan, with me, or with some other architect if you prefer it. Let us form a partnership together, subject to mutual arrangement for the remuneration of either ; my portion of the work being the constructional and æsthetic treatment of the art, based upon your practical knowledge of the costs and minutiæ of the materials. We will then build together

The sav-ing of the architect's per-cen-tage   for the client, and we shall be able to build for him much better and much cheaper, for, by virtue of our co-operation, and the system that I would have us work on, the whole of the architect's percentage will be saved him, in the mere saving of waste.

To state the case more forcibly, I will show this percentage, as saved in two halves, in this wise. Mr. Pushington, or the Board of Great Fadwell East, brings us a

140

job, let us say; how do we stand? You reckon so much per cent. on your capital, I the same on mine if I put any in. You reckon so much for your labour, I so much for mine. We then go into the costs together, I get out a drawing for the committee, and the contract is drawn up upon your quantities, in your and my name as one, or the name of our workshop, if you like, and there is no architect's percentage over, above, and on the costs. You know quite well, gentle Builder of Ideas, that the mere fact of our co-operation will save not only that half of my percentage which is taken as covering my design, but that I shall be as well paid, you will be well paid, and the return on our capital invested will remain the same. That is the first point in my proposal; that relates only to you and me. Now for my second, and the saving of the second half of the percentage, the half which is taken as covering my superintendence. This will be harder for you, and relates to the other workmen besides you and me. We will make of our workshop an industrial partnership. We will take all our men on at the Trade Union rates, drawing them, in fact, from the different Unions, and they shall not be our men, but the men of the workshop of which you and I are the pioneers. We shall then, after determining the rate or scale at which you and I are to be paid, the one for the earnings of management, the other for constructional design, sweep all the profits, over, and above the percentage on capital, not into our own pockets, as you, for instance, are doing now, but into a common workshop fund, for distribution amongst all the men, calculated by scale on their wages and the length of their service. Furthermore, we shall make rules for the future consolidation of our workshop. Every workman not only may, but shall, be a holder of capital up to a certain sum, and no workman shall be entitled to full workshop privileges, until he has worked for us, on trial, for at least three months, or draw profits until he has standing to the credit of his name on the books a reserve sum of at least £25. If you tell me that this cannot be done, I answer it has already, in several cases, been done, and works most wisely and well, it only needs the man to do it, perhaps you are, after all, not the Builder of Ideas !*

By co-operation among architect, builder, and workmen

The system of the co-operative workshop

---

* The factory Woodhouse Mills of Mr. George Thomson, at Huddersfield, is an instance in point. The system is also the one in force at the Guild of Handicraft.

I know it is a hard thing, this, I ask of you, and also of your architect ally ; it is nothing more nor less than inviting us both to professionally commit suicide. I, the architect, am to surrender my percentage on the costs, and my proud and superior special-pedestal position, you, the builder, are to have your earnings of management regulated by a force out of your own control, and have your master's hand a little tied. To begin with, we shall probably both of us lose, we shall be misunderstood by the men; we shall also be boycotted by the profession, the trade, and the building papers ; but, in the end, we, and all those working with us, will, without doubt, be great gainers, because the middle man's portion of both you and me will be got rid of, and, by the spirit and interest of our workmen, we shall reap other results unimagined. There is one thing, however, that we shall gain for the Art and Craft of Building, that will be worth all that we may lose or gain for ourselves. Have you ever considered what a disregard and waste of tradition is implied in the system, whereby one architect employs a variety of different builders, and often builders with whom he has never worked before, and may never work again ? By the nature of the system, this further means the employment of a number of different workmen, also continually changing. The builder, the architect, and the men are all new to each other, they have no cohesion, and what element of tradition there is in the workshop practice of all and each is constantly tending to disappear. I want, you and me, gentle Builder of Ideas, to re-construct the workshop, on the basis of a possible and continuing tradition. Let us, and our men, get to know each other's ways : let our plasterers get into the knack of knowing how I want my cornices to break round the window architraves, and my bricklayers, from experience of working with me, how I like my arches to rake, and my smiths to remember that I always swear when they file fine the edges of my scrolls, and my joiners to have sympathy with the particular ogee that I affect on the top of a frieze rail. Think of the cupboardsfull of needless drawings this would save me, the endless instructions it would save you, and the little varieties of interested responsibility it would leave to these same plasterers and bricklayers, smiths and joiners. Some firms, you know, as it is, pride themselves on getting into the ways of particular architects,

Its results on the traditions of the craft

142

but you, and those who have any workshop experience, know perfectly well that this can only be done by virtue of the men that they employ. And, I go further yet; it is not from vanity of my own style that I want my plasterers, and bricklayers, smiths, and joiners, to be in sympathy with me, but because, by this sympathy, and owing to the fact of our continuous co-operation, I shall become the vessel through which the tradition of our re-constructed workshop is to flow.

Imagine a number of architects, each with their own workshop, their group or guild of workmen around them, working continuously together, what style should we not develope? Each group its own, owing to the individuality of the men expressing itself in the details; for though the workshop will always need its architect or constructive designer, our newer system of responsible co-operation will inevitably approximate to the mediæval guild system, in which the workman was enabled to put his own individuality into his work.

When Mr. Pushington did me the honour of inviting me to build the new stables at his place in Berkshire, he asked, knowing that I had ideas on these matters, whether I cared to suggest any more satisfactory method than the customary one, for my own professional remuneration, and for the contract of the work. ^{Mr. Push-ington always to the point}

"I don't like the way you architects are paid," he said, and I replied that the percentage on the cost was a professional *bête noir* of mine.

So we agreed, after I had worked him out the plans of a building, costing about £2,500, that my honorarium should amount to £150, inclusive of travelling expenses, and that there should be nothing on extras. He, further, very gracefully offered me half of anything I might save him over the contract price, £2,500, within the sum of £3,000, which was the outside limit—all told—to which he wanted to go. This, however, I declined, as not being strictly professional; I venture to think, too, that, as a work of Art, the building was, in the end, the better for it.

Before we closed, however, Mr. Pushington made me a further suggestion.

"I do not wish," he said, to put this work out to competitive tender if I can help it, and I like to encourage novelties; you, my young friend, have cranks; are there any particular builders or workmen with whom you would like the work placed?"

"You, Mr. Pushington," I replied, "have men—I have not yet found any builder of Ideas—would it not be possible for Messrs. Sky Sign and Co. to supply us with men, material, everything?"

Yet
curiously
timid

"Yes, perhaps—but no, I'm afraid that's a bit impracticable,— no, perhaps we'd better do it in the usual way."

So it resolved itself into our employing the customary local builder, and I had all the bother of seeing that the lime was properly slacked, and the hoop iron properly oiled and sanded, and the mortar properly proportioned, etc., etc., etc., in short, that all the jargon of the specification was correctly carried out. How I longed for my builder of Ideas! and I vowed I would not rest till I found him.

Now, I think I know what you are going to say, and I will anticipate your criticism. You are not unnaturally going to argue that the cost of carriage, and transit of men, plant, and materials, will make this impracticable, and

Local
building

you will say, therefore, that local builders must be employed, and that the architect, hence, inevitably remain, owing to the fundamental pecuniary needs of the case, dissociated from the builder's yard, from the workshop.

My answer is—first, that it is right and proper that building should be done locally, good and spirited building can be done in no other way but locally, and by the men who understand the wants and ways of the neighbourhood, not the architect from London, who has, perhaps, even made his competition drawings without having inspected the site. Where contracts can be undertaken by firms at a distance, as at present, under a wasteful system, the same work can be done under an economical one. Furthermore, if the system I suggest is to have any efficacy at all, it will act in country districts, just as much as in the great Wen, in fact it will be easier, I think, to establish, in the country, where old workshop traditions still linger, and methods are less complex. It need not, however, act to the destruction of the eminent architect from London, in the event of his being really needed. You forget the enormous facility of locomotion placed at our disposal. It is much easier and cheaper now to move men, plant, material, to and

144

fro, than it was twenty years ago, and it will daily tend to become easier still. What I insist on, however, is, that if the London architect is to come, his own group of men shall come with him, and that the Guild, of which he is the centre, shall leave its mark upon the building to be erected.

In this again, we should have an approximation to what Guild was done by the mediæval builders, when the Guild travelled building from place to place. If there was a piece of work to be done that overtaxed the capacities of the local workmen, a neighbouring Guild was invited, and the masons, with the master mason, from Bury St. Edmunds, from Norwich, from Canterbury, would take up their sojourn at the Abbot's workshop.

The idea that the architect shall become his own con-tractor is not a new one, no less a person than Sir Charles Barry supported it many years ago, but the time was not ripe for it then ; architectural professionalism had not fully A wasted developed itself, nor had Trade Unionism, and the thing tradition was impossible then, in Barry's day, even had he been the man to do it. It is only now possible, by a frank recognition of the Trade Unionist and co-operative principles, by the architect. It was this that Barry and Pugin, who worked with him on the Houses of Parliament, had, owing to the circumstances of their time, no insight into, and the magnificent work they did, in training up a body of workmen for, and on, that great building, was practically thrown away in its large bearing on the craft of building, for want of an understanding of that workshop cohesiveness, that co-operative tradition, which we, of a late day, must make for in our policy of workshop re-construction.

I know an old gentleman in Mile End—an octogenarian mason, with both legs in the grave, for he carves nothing but tombstones,—who was trained by Pugin in the West-minster work. He looks back to it as a sort of golden age —it was the time he got real nice work to do,—but what has come out of it ? There was no effort made to hold the men together, beyond the immediate cash nexus of the contract, and when the great job was done they all drifted apart. Pugin's preaching of mediævalism, and Barry's ideas for the development of contract, were all futile and to no purpose, *for want of an understanding of the social*

145

and constructive side of the workshop. The whole tradition was wasted, and my old friend threw his chisel on one side and went into the tombstone line. He now walks about, a small, a very small, master, in a long, a very long, black coat, and a very tall top hat, looks like a mute, swears at the indifference of the workmen he employs, but still he does not forget the golden age.

But it is just the men of the golden age that we want to create, only the golden age shall last—shall indeed outlive the contract. I repeat what I stated before, in my chapter on the architect and the workman, *we must take more responsibility for the men, less responsibility for the work.* The character in our bricks and mortar will rise, as the tone of our workshop rises. This dictum, gentle builder of Ideas, applies to you, just as much as to me, and my professional colleagues. Suppose, now, you try to reconstruct your Building business in the way I have suggested—suppose we co-operate? I hold out my hand to you!

CHAPTER 14.—THE ART AND TECHNICAL IN-STRUCTOR OF TO-DAY, AND THE LITTLE CITIZEN OF THE FUTURE.

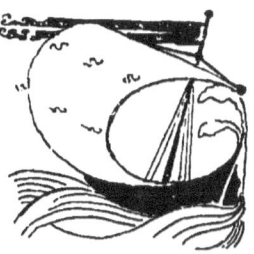

These more special considerations in the re-construction of the Workshop, through my own craft, have taken me away from the little citizen of the future. He it is to whom some day we have to look for the re-birth of that spirit which prompted Arnolfo's document; it is he who is to "proceed in the management of our affairs," so that our "magnanimity and wisdom" as a "people of noble origin" may be "evinced in our outward acts." I would, therefore, dedicate this chapter to Jack, and also to the man in whose hands for the moment his artistic and technical teaching is entrusted. This man is the "Technical and Art instructor," a special new breed of teacher, who is neither of the workshop nor of the school, but invented by these supplementary technical institutions for the well-being of the new citizenship.

I will tell you the sort of man you are creating,—when I say *you*, I mean the political gentlemen who act on County Council Technical Sub - Committees, and, without much practical knowledge, do conscientiously try to do something for the improvement of Art in its application to Industry. I will ask you to take this from an expert, whose study has been the re-construction of the Workshop, and the training of its men. I will tell you, gentlemen, the sort of man you are producing, and then you may be inclined to piously breathe with me that the South Kensington system, with its certificated paper men, and its stately Mummy, had its merits after all, and that the last state of the Art instructor shall be worse than the first.

He is, to begin with, a man of strictly commercial instincts, who takes up what he would call "a line," he does the thing *first* for shekels; this is no matter if he does it well, but he does not do it well, for he is usually a man who has found that some other line does not pay so well as "Art teaching." He is drawn from various social circles. Sometimes he is an artizan who has fallen out with his Union, and drifted away from the bench; sometimes he is an elementary teacher, with endless qualifications; sometimes he is a City clerk, with whom money is no consideration, but who finds "Art teaching" more lucrative than double entry; more frequently he is a commercial traveller with a varied experience,—boots, timber, artificial teeth, baby linen, what you will. He has good address, wears a good coat, writes a good letter, and impresses you favourably, especially if you are a committee, with a sense of practical competence and energy; and he is always up to date. But, with all these good qualities, he lacks just those one or two best qualities that shall fit him for the work he ought to do.

It is inevitable that the artificial and supplementary system of art and technical teaching, which we are estabish-ing all over the country, should also lead to the creation of an artificial and unnecessary Art teacher. When the system of teaching is outside the Workshop, the teacher must be outside the Workshop likewise, and become divorced from what he is proposing to teach.

The three kinds of Technical and Art Education — Now, there are two kinds of technical education, as com-monly understood, and of these, in so far as they bear upon Art, Craft and Industry, the one is as valueless as the other is important. The one is the teaching, in evening art classes, to all sorts and conditions of men, the other is the training of the children and teachers in the elements of handicraft. Of the first, we have enough and to spare; indeed, an over-abundance of what is, except from a social and recreative point of view, all but valueless; of the other we have as yet only a limited quantity, and that inefficiently administered. But there is yet another sort of technical education, which is more important than either, and of which, at present, we have, in the largest sense, nothing at all.

Those who have followed me thus far, will see at once that I refer to the teaching in the Workshop by the work-men, to technical education, as it was understood by the mediæval guilds and in the Workshop of the Renaissance, technical education, that recognises no teaching, where the teaching function is divorced from the workshop function. This genuine teaching is dependent on workshop re-con-struction, and I look to Jack Trudge, not Thomas Trudge, but Jack, his first-born, some day, to do it. As for the second kind of technical teaching, that of the child, and his teacher in the elements, that we may in part leave to Timothy Thumbs, it is the work of the educationalist, rather than the Workshop; though the Workshop also, here, should have a voice in its practical direction, for the Workshop of the future is implied in it; and as to the teaching of Art, to all sorts and conditions of men, let us give it up as Art, it will not help us to reconstruct the Workshop; let us regard it as recreative or social only, for it is of no other value. The need for a little more genuineness, in this respect, was brought home to me once, in the earlier days, before I had expressed myself too definitely to the Rev. Simeon Flux, as to the value of his efforts for the æsthetic sub-consciousness of Great Fadwell East, and when he and I were yet allies. He asked me once, and the honour was a distinguished one to an unknown young man, to judge the awards in one of his local Art Exhibitions. What he needed, he said, was " An expert to help him, an independent opinion, especially an architect's, it would be invaluable, *and*," he added, incidentally, "it may help *you*, four thousand circulars will go out with your name on them, the press will be invited, and Lady Sophia Bindles will give the prizes on your award." So the æsthetic sub-consciousness of Great Fadwell East was displayed before me in groups, one Easter time, in St. Saviour's schools. There were arrays of chip-carved stools, and walls full of fretwork brackets, repoussé copper ash trays no end, brass finger plates for imaginary doors, and pinched iron work for no imaginary purpose at all, and as to the embossed leather work, the hides of so many beeves would have covered Carthage many times. I had not expected much, but this was less than I had even dreamed of, and a spirited dialogue took place, between the Rector and me, in the vestry.

The Rev. Simeon Flux, and the first kind of Technical Education

" Really, Mr. Flux, I cannot award prizes to some of these groups, they are too bad."

" Oh! but, my dear fellow, on their merits, you know, on their merits; you must not judge them by your own standard! "

" But then they have no merits at all, absolutely none; what in the world is the good of all this miserable fretwork? "

" The good? " said the Rector, and he looked at me reproachfully, " Isn't it good that these fellows should be taught to use their hands, isn't it good that they should be given some interest in their colourless lives, isn't it good that they should be kept from loafing up and down the Horwark Highway, and won from the public-houses, surely it isn't for *you* to judge of what good all this may be accomplishing, *that*," he added, with a smile that turned off his justifiable anger at my impertinence, "*that* is the business of the Rector, not of the Artist."

" But then," I insisted, " that is just the point, I'm not here to say what good the work does, but whether it is good in itself."

The Rector laid his hand on my arm very calmly, but very firmly, and, as he led me to one of the groups, quoted a most musical and ambiguous passage from Ruskin, which I cannot now remember, because it was open to so many constructions, and contained all the ethics of Art ; and before I had time to reply, he had taken a slip of paper from his pocket, scribbled something on it and handed it to me.

"Yes," he said, "they're all very bad, but I take your meaning, I *quite* take your meaning—will this suit you?"

"THE JUDGE, IN AWARDING THE FIRST PRIZE TO NO. 4 OF THIS GROUP, RECOMMENDS THE PUPILS TO TURN THEIR ENERGIES TO OTHER FORMS OF HANDICRAFT BESIDES FRETWORK."

Those who are acquainted with the Rev. Simeon Flux on committees or in private life, his prompt, masterful, persuasive way of going to work, will know how impossible it is to cope with him on his own ground. I made my stand, but was completely routed, and so, in the end, Lady Sophia Bindles gave the biggest prizes, on my award, to George Grubbins, the local grocer, because he was the most regular church-goer ; the Rev. Simeon Flux and the æsthetic sub-consciousness of Great Fadwell East, expressed themselves highly satisfied with my discrimination ; the Lady Sophia Bindles bought ten guineas' worth of Fretwork, which her splendid footman carried off in a hamper, and the Pressmen quoted from the end of the Rev. Simeon Flux's peroration : "Beauty is Truth, Truth Beauty, that is all, etc., etc., etc." On the whole it was a most successful function.

Well, there we have it, the Rev. Simeon Flux has carried this first kind of technical education to its highest finish. He has reduced it to its primal element, a purely social and recreative one. It has nothing to do with the Workshop at all, and does nothing at all for Industry ; it keeps the boys from the public houses and Mr. George Grubbins at Church, both things, doubtless, much to be wished for, but neither of them of any direct value for our national development in Art, Craft and Industry, and whether it be done in the Rev. Simeon Flux's evening classes, or at the Upper Galore Polytechnic, the object, though an excellent one, is the same, and we must not misunderstand it, or imagine, that by state-aiding it, we are thereby helping to directly improve our national production. We may be doing lots of excellent things, but we are not doing what we think we are doing, and want to do.

With our second kind of teaching, the case is different, here we tap another vein of the national organism, and here,

too, the promiscuous Art instructor is not wanted. The
teaching of the child in the school is important. It is in
the school, before the age of 14, that the little citizen will
have fashioned for him his fundamental capacities for the
understanding of form, mass, line, colour, music, his
appreciation for landscape, and his delight in the human
body; all these should be instilled into him first in the
school. The scope for the elements of technical and artistic
teaching in the school is infinite; but, be it always
remembered, the training here must be a very different
thing from the technical training which the Art instructor
and the like are called upon to give. It is the training in
the use of the coloured chalks that we want here, a training
very simple, very large, and, before all things, very human.

Timothy Thumbs, and the second kind of Technical Education

Timothy Thumbs once, but only once, had an idea of
giving up his appointment under the Great Fadwell East
Board, and becoming an Art teacher in the "technical
education movement." There seemed more scope, more
leisure, or, as he expressively put it—

"You do your six-months work for a County Council, and
have the other six months to loaf; the pay is more for six
months than the Board gives me for twelve. I'm sick of
all this dreary grind and drive; and just think what I might
do for the old boys' club!"

But I vetoed the idea on the ground that the new
occupation was not sufficiently genuine.

"I don't think these jobs," said I, "should be undertaken
by men unless they have a sheet anchor. The only justifi-
cation for the Art instructor is that he is either constructing
in the workshop, *i.e., an artizan*, or creating in the school,
i.e., a practising schoolmaster; if you resign your appointment, you cut your sheet anchor. Besides, don't you believe
you'll keep the old boys' club thereby, it will just go to pot,
and then what will there be worth living for in life?"

I am glad to think that, in return for the many things I
owe to him, Timothy Thumbs should at least owe this to
me, that he still holds his appointment under the Board of
Great Fadwell East, grinding, mean and unsympathetic
though it is, and giving him no hope of an old age pension,
but just putting another man over his head when he's past
work. Timothy Thumbs now, amongst his other many jobs,
takes an evening class of boys at bench work, and he finds,
as he says, that "the little chaps like it, seem just cut out
for it, like ducks on the Lea,—they make their joints quite
as well as I do—it's a wonderful thing, the human hand,
when you come to think of it!"

And it is of those little chaps, who are budding out under the cramped but human influence of Timothy Thumbs, that we are to make our future citizens. They will find they owe much to Timothy Thumbs when they get to see it, but they might owe a good deal more if he were left a little freer to give that concrete, graphic, simple, human teaching, the real Technical Education for the school in which he has so much natural skill, but for which "My Lords," in their visible incarnation, never give him credit, and which cannot be tested by examinations and certificates.

The little citizen of the future and the third kind of Technical Education As for the third kind of Technical Education, the kind for which at present we do nothing—the education of the Workshop by the Workshop. I believe it is a thing that we shall come to, little by little, if we keep the need of it always before us; but the re-construction of the Workshop comes first, before we can bring the teaching function and the workshop function again together. In my chapter on the Metropolitan School of Architecture, I threw out some proposals as to how it could be done in one particular line, and in my suggestion for the application of it to Messrs. Sky Sign and Co.'s works, I pointed to its possible development there. In every Industry there are means and ways of doing it, if we were only bold enough to try them. I do not say the State should do it, that I leave to the politicians to decide : all that the educationalist need say is, that this particular thing, somehow or other, has got to be done.

But to return to the Art Instructor. I have an idea—it may be a somewhat fanciful one—that I should like to make an Art Instructor, of a different sort, of young Jack Trudge, the first-born of my friend. He is a bright-eyed lad of sixteen-and-a-half years, skilful with his fingers, but desperately casual, and, as often as not, when I want him particularly to come to an evening class, or an "Arts and Crafts" lecture, the young scapegrace prefers courting down the Mile End Road with Grace Giggle and Sybil Sillysweet. I don't think any the worse of him for that, it is probably much healthier, and certainly more human, than stewing in a lecture-room ; only I hope, and this I have plainly told him, that he will not too early try any practical refutation of the theory of Malthus. He has made his promise, and, to me at least, in all the big things of life, Jack always keeps his word.

Now I want to take him out of his workshop, where he is not happy, and place him, with a few other mates, into a shop where the conditions shall be more healthy and more hopeful; perhaps some day a few of my architectural

152

colleagues,—whose sphere of vision is not bounded only by the prospect of professional success, will help me accomplish this end. Meanwhile, I am having him trained in a fundamental understanding of the application of design to material in every sense, and what I would like to do, after letting him try his hand at as many different crafts as possible, tinkering if you like, and a veritable Jack-of-all-trades, just as your mediæval workman was in some Norfolk village by the sea, is to let him specialize at one thing only. Then I will try and get him to become a secretary or something to the branch of his Trade Union, to which he will in due course belong; before all things I insist on his retaining his membership in Timothy Thumbs' old boys' club, but in that I shall find no great difficulty. I may add that Mr. Thomas Trudge, though he laughs at my educational ideas, has given me *carte blanche* to do what I like with Jack's training, and whenever he sees Jack dropping off, or not acting on any of my most peculiar and incomprehensible fads, he just says to him, "You little fool, why don't you do as you're told"? Thus am I safeguarded on all sides, and may do something besides talking of the rights and duties of the citizen. But I want, as I said, to make (save the mark!) an "Art instructor" of Jack as well; and I shall do this by making a first-rate workman of him to begin with, and then, by broadening his sympathies, and drawing out of him, bit by bit, a few of those things for which I pleaded before, a little of the sense of Beauty, and the power to awaken it in others.

He shall, for instance, spend his Bank Holidays in Epping Forest or on the River, and not be told that it is immoral to travel or to enjoy himself on Sundays; he shall discuss, freely and frankly, questions of religion and physiology, and he shall be left to construct his own ethics for himself, on the basis of perfect personal freedom and his love for his friends. He shall be given some glimmerings of the Great History of his country and the duties of her workmen in the future. Then he and his mates shall be taught to play football and to row, indeed, enjoy all the pride and splendour, and without the crudeness, of the academic blazer. He shall sing an Elizabethan catch, in preference to caterwauling down Whitechapel; and, above all, get out as often as possible into the free sunshine, and enjoy the use of his naked limbs in air and water. Of politics and papers, debates, lectures and social questions, there will be enough and to spare from other people; I will let those come as they may, but not to hinder the larger affairs of life. I, at least, will do my best to educate out of him some of that sense which

L   153 shall make these larger affairs beloved and understood. Give me five years, and a little help now and again, when I ask for it, and Jack Trudge will be as ready to do good work in Education as any man living.

During the period of apprenticeship, however, and until the new citizen is ready, we must do what we can with the old one, and the Art and Technical instructor is still abundantly to hand. He appears before us, armed *cap-à-pie* with certificates, testimonials, diplomas, Ds., and degrees, tested to finest steel with examinations, and full of windy wisdom, but of little real knowledge, of no technical skill, of no creative power, of no enthusiasm for Beauty, and of little human sympathy. He comes to the Upper Galore Polytechnic, and takes his classes, where he teaches his lads, much as a butcher would cut up beeves, or a fly-catcher stick on flies, indeed, how should he do otherwise, poor man? You, by the system you have imposed upon him, have made it impossible for him to have any other interest than his monthly salary, you have rooted him out of his workshop, and kicked over his ideal of Education, if ever he had any; how can he help himself? You, Mr. Pushington, in conjunction with the County Councils and the School Boards, and the other inefficient educational agencies, all of you working blindly, if conscientiously, to *what* end, have created this man. Be proud of him! The constructive teaching in Art, Craft, and Industry for the twelve thousand souls of Great Fadwell East, you have placed in his hands; and the citizens of the future, who, besides their rights and duties, are presumably to have also creative capacities, and some sense of Beauty, are under his guidance.

No! Jack Trudge who, after working through his colourless day at the shop, and filling in his odd moments with the perusal of *Grits, Snap Shots, Pot-sherds*, and other affiliated papers of that genus, shall not be expanded and trained by him. I'll not have it. For, do you think the result will be altogether profitable to Jack Trudge? Do you think that this man, the Art instructor, is really going to help us in our task of workshop re-construction? I leave the answer to your good judgment, gentlemen!

154

CHAPTER 15.—ON JACK'S INITIATION INTO THE CITIZENSHIP.

The ideal of Jack's Citizenship still remains undefined. I think we had best leave it so. It will shape itself sure enough later. But might we not turn to something more hopeful than the flabby liberalism, which the middle and upper-class Englishman holds? You would not have Jack educated in Mr. Pushington's benevolent, but semi-cynical, nihilism, would you? For what is the position after all. It is not that he does not understand, but he is of a different time, another age. This being so, we may accord him his prerogative of unbelief.

"Your Utopia of a re-constructed State, built up by the producers, is a dream," he says, "it will all be wrecked ere it is half worked out; and why? because we are not isolated, because we are dependent on foreign conditions. What will happen? If we daily devote more of legislative and national attention to what you say, and perhaps, rightly, is more important, our social re-construction at home, and less attention to our Empire holding, and the position we assume abroad, we shall suddenly be called upon to choose between the two, and we shall choose the former; then the foreign conditions will tell, our prestige will be swept away. Follows the inevitable re-action, follows war, and perhaps defeat: the collapse of trade, on which, not only the re-construction, but the very construction itself of the Workshop depends, and we shall be thrown back a hundred years, and may begin re-constructing again—next time, perhaps, in earnest; but for the present—that will not be in my day," says Mr. Pushington, "therefore leave me alone."

This is pessimistic fatalism, and to this has the shallow and buoyant liberalism of the middle of this century been transformed. But if the Zeitgeist has made Mr. Pushington a pessimist, it has made Mr. Trudge the reverse. "I also do not care," says the latter, "but what I am doing, I have got to do; it may be an immediate interest, but it must be done; therefore, also leave me alone."

It has been my endeavour in these chapters to give some expression to the point of view of the producer in Industry, that of the producer in Art is better known to the polite public. But far down, underneath, the positions are the

Artist and Producer: their Idealism and Ethics

same, for Art, as I have insisted, is but the higher production. We pull ourselves up oftentimes, and ask, why do we go on, what is it all for ? This mere trifle of mine, of what use or beauty may it be, will it give any one delight ? May be not, may be it is useless and unlovely, and will give no man pleasure, what then ? Why just this, we are brought face to face with the ethics of production ; the artist producer stands forth. This trifle of mine is a mere symbol, the thing itself is empty, vain, its goodness consists in the spirit put into it, and the doing it, its creation by us, reflects a greater doing, symbolizes a creation elsewhere, in which we are sublimely and unconsciously taking part. We talk of a piece of machine-made work as soulless, what a deal we mean when we say that ! So let us continue to make our trifles, remembering always that they are symbols only. This, if you will, is the Idealists' Gospel of Work, and the strength of our continuance, is the measure of our Idealism. Artist and producer, then, have the same ethics, and just as it is the individual touches of the artist that make the great work of Art, so it is the little human details impressed upon production that give it interest or character. This, in our vast mechanical system of Industry and individualism, we have missed sight of. *Individualism* has lost us *Individuality*. Individuality has gone out of Industry, but it must be brought back again. The system has destroyed the things created, and in destroying the productions we destroy the producers. Lower the standard of the work and you lower the standard of the man. But detail after detail we have got to re-conquer. Is it more likely that Mr. Push-ington, or Mr. Trudge, will win this battle for us ? Neither, you say ? Then I pin my faith on Jack. In the wisdom of Solomon we find aptly stated the position of modern individualism, with its irresponsible wielding of the instru-ments of production. " Fodder, a wand, and burdens, are for the ass; food, correction, and work, are for the servant "; but one of the Prophets replies to the sneer of the cynic, and answers for modern labour, with its pleading for the recognition of the standard of life, and its half defined, perhaps impossible, ideal of a collectivist state, " Pay me my price, if not, forbear, and God be with thee."

Envoi to Mr. Push-ington

It has been cast in my teeth that I do not really praise Mr. Pushington, but poke fun at him. Far be it from me to do anything so uncourteous, for this would surely be both unfair and ill-mannered on my part. No, Mr. Pushington and I are the best of friends, and though we differ on many

156

vital questions, no one so fully recognises his worth and helpfulness to the community as I do. Indeed, I may honestly say, that any public utterances I may have ventured upon him have had his fullest sanction, with one exception only—my praise of him. This his modesty has always held in check. And if there be critics who have said "Yes, but how do you make him appear before us ? You draw him as a 'bourgeois,' a man half-hearted in social questions, a plutocrat, who is wasting his money for publicity, when he might spend it with wiser thought for public purposes, a man who has in him all the culture and unbelief of these latter days, and of an apparent but no real appreciation for what you call the 'Sense of Beauty.'"

I can only say, I am sorry if that is the impression I have given of him. Emphatically no, Mr. Pushington is not the vulgar plutocrat, not the self-made man, not the iron king of a bygone generation, and if he *is* a little lacking in that Idealism of the earlier part of this century, which gave the heroic touch to the self-made business man of forty years ago, the Idealism that Tennyson has left us in Locksley Hall the first, and which we might call the Crystal Palace Idealism of 1851, he is, on the other hand, much more all round in his sympathies, and, as I said, believes in "Tendency," though he is, with justice, suspicious of social panaceas. Before all things, he is frank in his beliefs and unbeliefs. He has said "Yes, I am what you socialists call a 'Bourgeois.' I believe that the whole industrial system is suffering transformation, perhaps going to pieces ; I mistrust Trade Unions, I object to 'agitators,' but I always vote solid with my party, and I find time from my political labours to read the Fabian essays and William Morris's books, what more do you want ? "

I will ask the critics to bear in mind that this man is the head of one of the greatest business houses in the world, that he has practically endowed one of the largest polytechnics in England, that he finances one of the leading liberal journals, that much private bill legislation is due to his energy, and that his annual purchases at the Royal Academy are a constant source of consideration to artists. Surely no imaginary humour of mine would hurt him, nor does he need any praise it might be in my power to bestow.

Similarly, I have been told that my introduction of so eminent a divine as the Rev. Simeon Flux into these essays, is in questionable taste, and I have been asked by a mutual friend to change the name and introduce him in disguise, as it were. But I have not seen the need of this,

The raison d'être of the Rev. Simeon Flux

and I do not think the Rev. Simeon will, in the least, mind what I say of him. Public men are fair game, and one might introduce Lord Salisbury or Lord Rosebery into an industrial situation, did occasion need it. The Rev. Simeon is a wise man, too, and knows that I take him as a type; the type of many of those who are conscientiously endeavouring to graft Culture on to Industry from above, and, in his case, through the Church. There are many who give up their lives to this end, and, doubtless, it will be counted to them for righteousness. To talk of workshop re-construction, however, or of the shaping of the Ideal of the future citizenship, without taking this type into consideration, would surely be one-sided. The Rev. Simeon Flux is, what Blake would have called, "an energy," and the poet might have met him in Heaven or Hell, alternately, as it suited his purpose.

Mr. Trudge, as a person, is less known to the polite world, and he merely shrugged his shoulders and laughed when I asked him if he minded my putting him into a book. "You see," I said, "I want to be honest; it's no good my saying these things about people that don't really exist, is it? So if a man comes to me, and says ' That's not true,' shall you mind if I refer him your way? "

Mr. Trudge's common sense

Mr. Trudge did not mind; why should he? I do not think he will bother to read the book, and in that he is quite right. His world is one quite separate and apart, and when he does appear in any way publicly, he appears as what *The Times* would call "an agitator," and no letters from him would be inserted in its columns under any pretext whatever.

Timothy Thumb's apology

Friendship alone, and my sympathy with his militancy, have accorded me all the pardon I need ask of Mr. Timothy Thumbs. " I feel we are working to the same end," he said to me, "so do just as you like about it; I only wish more of our fellows could be got to look at things in the same way." A few days later he sent me the following letter which, with his leave, I quote in full :—

" The more I think over what you have written about the elementary teacher, the more I like it. Every elementary teacher I have met with in literature, up to now, has been either an ass or a humbug, perhaps both. Now, I think you have hit the key-note of our being. We really want our children to rise up and bless us; to feel that their lives are a bit fuller for having known us. None are better aware than we, how clumsily we got about this, and how terribly hampered we are, not only by unsympathetic authorities, but by absolutely hostile ones. Consider the training most of us have had—from early youth, under the blighting influence of the Church! At the age when you and your friends began to drink of the waters of life at Cambridge or Oxford, we were *being trained* at a Church College. Do you know what that means? Have you ever tried to realize? If not, before you go to print, read dear old Jimmy Runciman's 'Schools and Scholars.'

"In thinking over your chapters the other night, and your description of our puny efforts to educate the Sense of Beauty in our little ones, a school, not far from here, rose up before me. If you will visit it in the summer months, you will find the whole of the corridors one mass of bloom. You will find, in the boys department alone, between two and three hundred plants, all tenderly cared for, and belonging to the children, each child tending its own, and you will find the master one of the best of men. This is his idea of encouraging his little ones to make their own surroundings beautiful. Nor is this an isolated case, I could take you to dozens of schools where this is done—you see it doesn't cost much!"

I think that letter rings true.

As for Mr. Pennyworth, he merely remarked, "If the chief has no objection, I really don't see why I should; in fact, I don't think that it makes much difference one way or the other—it won't affect the friendly relations between him and me." ^{Mr. Penny-worth's in-difference}

So I have made my peace with my little world of friends, and as I never propose to stand for Great Fadwell East in any public capacity, do not expect any unpleasant con-sequences from being outspoken. You see the types are only types, and the re-construction of the workshop is going on silently and quite surely, whether they or I wish it, or say anything for or against.

The ideal of Jack's citizenship will then, as I have said, shape itself, but I should like here to offer a few more considerations towards its shaping. Throughout these chapters I have dwelt but little on the great question of human relationship—the bearing of individuals to one another. I would prefer to leave that for later and closer consideration elsewhere, in another volume perhaps, but inasmuch as it is the corner stone of all workshop

ON JACK'S INITIATION INTO THE CITIZENSHIP.

re-construction, and all building up of citzenship, it may
not be omitted.

The new basis of the Work-shop We need something, not so much in place of the moral
basis upon which the mediæval workshop was constructed,
but something that shall give it practical expression in a
modern manner. We need a vehicle, as it were, to carry
those simple Christian maxims upon which each democratic
movement is ever harking back. This, I believe, we shall
find, in a freer, more direct, more genuine relationship
between human beings, and the fresher atmosphere of the
re-constructed workshop will make this possible.

Just as, in distribution, we have to set aside the artificial
relations that have grown up between producer and consumer, so in production, and in the education of citizenship,
we have to arrive at a more genuine and intimate relationship
between human beings. The re-constructed Workshop
must have this for its basis ; here will be the faith of the
little citizen of the future. So personal is this question, that
it seems out of place in any consideration of the action of
men together for any public purpose. But it is just because
The basis of com-radship or the human bond it is so personal that it is so important. At present, where
men are bound together in production, their bond is one of
chance, or of common enmity to an employer, and they
become friends *because* they are shopmates. In the re-constructed Workshop this will have to be inverted, and they
will become shopmates rather *because* they are friends.
Here, once again, is the unit ; we come back to that. It is
the unit, the individual, that we have got to touch.

Somewhat, in this way, might we state our belief.

That moment when the hand of my friend was pressed in
mine, has expanded over my life, and become it. The
reason why I choose you—what is it ? Let us call it a two-
fold reason. First, because of the you in you, second,
because of the you in me ; the first in your own character
and choosing ; the second, the magnetic force of which I am
the vessel ; the first in your own making, the second entrusted
to me by God. It is not new in itself ; this, the feeling
that drew Jesus to John, or Shakespeare to the youth of
the sonnets, or that inspired the friendships of Greece, has
been with us before, and in the new citizenship we shall
need it again. The Whitmanic love of comrades is its
modern expression, Democracy—as socially, not politically,
conceived—its basis. The thought as to how much of the
solidarity of labour and the modern Trade Union movement may be due to an unconscious faith in this principle

160

of comradeship, is no idle one. The freer, more direct, and more genuine, relationship between men, which is implied by it, must be the ultimate basis of the re-constructed Workshop. "When I touch the human body," said Novalis, "I touch Heaven!"

This relationship—*human bond*—as distinguished from the cash or other nexus, we have to study, to analyse, to find, if possible, the philosophic basis of, and we may learn in teaching it. We have to train ourselves and those we teach, to lay high stakes on new personalities, to strive for infalli-bility of decision, and instant decision when a new personality comes. I look into your eyes, stranger; God grant me the power of instantly telling whether or not you are sent for me. A few times wrong, and we grow sensitive to right choosing, each right choice makes the next more certain. This magnetism of the human bond, too, is generative, you light me, and the fire grows within me, I spread it, and it grows again, till at last the whole air in which we move is charged with it. It runs into us, and through us, again and again; as we receive more, we emit more, till our whole surroundings grow brilliant with light—that incom-prehensive blue light in the visions of Heinrich von Ofterdingen.

Much of this will, doubtless, appear fanciful, especially when read in the irony of existing conditions; polite society with its artificial barriers, industrial life, conducted on the assumption that the interests of masters and men, the interests that make for production, are antagonistic. Those of us who are teaching—or rather creating to a newer purpose, will seek, however small, to make a wider field. The human bond, we shall insist, must enter into Industrial life, it must be the key of the artist-workman's existence: his faith.

A faith, however, is not a thing that can or need be expressed. How unsatisfying, unscientific, inartistic, appear all expositions of faith where given in allegory. There is a poetical fustiness about them all. They stink of stale perfumery. Comte, the philosopher, may have been wonder-ful, but Babick, the fanatic, "*barbier et fusionist*," who sought to inspire the Paris Commune of 1871, with his new universal religion of "Fusionism," was more wonderful still. To the artist, the higher producer, is given the privilege of allegory, he takes the place of the priest, and, inasmuch as he refrains from foisting definition upon others, he prays for freedom of individuality for himself. When the time comes, the allegory will find itself, and the artist-producer, its exponent, will, doubtless, be at hand; for the present we may leave it. Faith, like Art, can bide its time.

But now, given Jack his comradeship, I would still like to regard him with the eye of the higher producer in the re-constructed Workshop; would find yet another thing for the ideal of his citizenship to shape itself upon. Say he is constructing with his hands, engaged on anything in the Whitmanic catalogue of trades, in which head and hand work together, to do this rightly, we must fire three things within him, the *quality of Reverence, the regard for Tradition, the sense of Creation.* In our national life of to-day, we have lost the first, we ignore the second, and we are groping after the third. What shall we give him to reverence? where are our traditions? how shall he create?

The basis of Reverence, of Tradition, of Creation

"In the reverence of God," thus begins old Cennino Cennini's treatise on painting, "In the reverence of God, and of the Virgin Mary, and of St. Eustachius, and of St. Francis, and of St. John the Baptist, and of St. Anthony of Padua, and generally of all the saints of God!" That was the *Faith.* Then, with the same breath, he continues, "and in the reverence of Giotto, of Taddeo, and of Agnolo, the master of Cennino," that was the *Workshop.* He is about to create something, his gage is tradition, felt from master to pupil, his motive power is reverence, the *Faith* and the *Workshop* are inseparable.

In accordance with the power and dignity of our imaginations, shall we reverence, and in like manner is tradition illuminated by imagination, it is expanded and unfolded by it. By imagination the humanities of the past come near to us and touch us, their strength grows stronger and into us, their light more vivid and around us. They aid us to move from present, by help of past, into future; they help us to be human, and to be human is to come very near creating. Let but Jack imagine these three—reverence, tradition, creation, and there will be food enough for their nourishment. For modern England has had her great men, her poets, her artists, her scientists, her mechanicians, her in-breathers; and, in accordance with the labour enthusiasm plus the human enthusiasm, in each is reverence due. For tradition, we need but train him to look back; as for reverence, we teach him to look around, and the whole fair field of history lies open behind him : England, with her cycles of civilization, each built upon the last, and each retrospecting to one still

162

earlier, shall be the landscape that we set before him. Stern old Bess of Hardwicke shall come to him on a fair morning in the Peak country, and he shall listen, with the monks, for the chisel of William of Sens in the choir of Canterbury Cathedral. Think of this, and then of a little English boy I met the other day—fresh from the Board School, one among many, perhaps, who had never heard of Nelson! As for creation, there is the future for Jack. Get him but to feel that he is the centre of some growing organism, and straightway the world begins anew. Our creative instinct is proof of our divine origin; let him but realize of what he is the symbol, as he models the clay, or hammers the metal, and we set the seal of the divine enthusiam upon him for ever.

This I would call the educational ideal from the point of view of the higher production, the point of view of the artist.

We need not, I think, concern ourselves with the question as to whether the higher production, the Art movement of to-day, is unreal or not, an affectation, the plaything of a leisured class, as William Morris would have it, even for his own tapestries and books. An Art movement is judged by its men, and at the bottom of all lies character, individual character—the unit again. Earnest men and honest work make an art movement, and its relative greatness, to other times, is in the number of earnest men it tells, and the amount of honest work it does; not the work of stars, they may shine forth always and in the dark, but of the divine average. It was that that made great the art of Greece, and mediæval Europe; I, for one, do not believe that an Art movement can be judged by any other standard than the character of the men in it, and the consequent stamp they leave on its productions; and, in spite of all he says, William Morris is one of my own thirty-nine artistic articles.

I would like, however, to say a few words at parting, on the personal development of my little citizen, on the self-centredness. I would see in him another quality yet, in addition to his power of comradeship. The basis of Individuality

One of the greatest glories of the century is its intellectual diversity; and we may receive proudly the gibe of the Oriental on the cultured Englishman, that the Sahibs have each their own God. I can imagine no more splendid basis for a large constructive social policy than the self-centredness of the individual, it is as the well pounded particles of concrete laid by the builder in foundation for the stately stone-work of his house.

Upon the recognition of this individuality, together with the faith of comrades, we may commence the shaping of our ideal of citizenship. For my own part I would like to see the Catholic Church, one and undivided, assume again the position it occupied in the time of the early renaissance, when it accepted Hellas, and accepted Dante ; the church as Pico della Mimandola, or our own Sir Thomas More would have conceived it ; divested of the colossal worldliness and vice of its Medicis and Borgias, and before the theological specialization of Luther and Calvin, or the counter-reformation of Rome. But the universalism of this century makes for a yet larger and more generous conception, and postulates the recognition of each man's individuality.

The consideration of this is a constant problem to the artist ; whether the full recognition of individuality is compatible with large corporate action, and social legislation, government, collectivism, the tyranny of majorities, socialism, whatever for the moment we elect to call it. I admit the danger, and see its seriousness, but it does not seem to affect the question ; we must not let thought of the danger confuse the issues. If I watch the stream of tendency aright, it is making for two things simultaneously : the need for corporate action in our re-constructed state, and the need for fullest individuality in our future citizen, the one must be the complement of the other. Whitman strikes the note in his " Personalism " of Democracy, and his much jeered at strings of trades. Doubtless they are wearisome, those long catalogues of the occupations of uninteresting people, and Democracy *is* wearisome, it is so insignificant in its largeness, so common-place, so inconspicuous. But Democracy, and the poet's rendering of it, are at one, and we must not miss the point. The poet states them neither as rhythmical cadences, nor as truths of life ; they are all there on the chance, the slender chance, that your little creative bit, your tiny trifle of sub-divided occupation, may be among them ; he is careless of form, if he can but take you by the hand, and, for your part, you forgive him all the tedium, if you light on that one little clause and comfort for your own individuality—his particular thought of you.

As the poet's hint, so is Democracy itself. It is not great for its largeness, but for these very details of personalism, which it makes possible, and which are so dull to you and me, if we do not feel them, yet so tremendous when they become part of our lives. We cannot take Democracy, with a big D, by the hand, or endow Humanity with a consciousness, even if we call it Christ, for the purpose of our soul's satisfaction, but we can find what we seek in some one particular human being. "When I touch the human body," says Novalis, " I touch Heaven."

This then may be our inspiration, and starting from this standpoint, the recognition of individuality on the basis of comradeship, those of us who are striving to create for the future of national character, must seek for the mean in harmonious education, for we must train our little citizen harmoniously if we would shape his ideal aright. What a superb creature might not the modern Englishman or greater Englander become ! To us, teachers and artists, is entrusted the care of his forming. Think what he has behind him, and what it has been given him to form his character upon. The study of the classics and of Greek athleticism, we might get from our public schools, Then comes the Spirit of the Renaissance, at which our modern, mental freedom may catch with delight, had it but a little more understanding of the sense of Beauty. Our contact with India yields the large passive basis of oriental mysticism, and, in the Workshop, slowly re-con-structing, continually reverting, yet never returning to the mediæval ideal of the state regulated standard of life, the conception of Democracy as a social order. The forming of such a man will set the type for our ideal of citizenship, and to him will be given the comprehension of Art as the crown and fulfilment of national life. It is only in the re-constructed Workshop that we may hope to find our citizen perfected in heart, and hand, and head, and Beauty ; and it is through the Workshop, its steady and gradual re-construction, and by keeping ever before us this new purpose in our ideal of citizenship, that we can get nearer to our end. As for Art, the higher production, it is but the crown and fulfilment of noble citizenship. It can bide.

I was watching, the other day, the lilies making their way up through my garden. It is a London garden, so at its best there is not much to be expected from it, but on looking closely I found, that by some accidental shifting of the soil, all the bulbs had got covered up with much more mould

The citizen of the future

165

than they could bear, and, unburying the surface, I saw leaf after leaf, pale and colourless, thrown off underground, and a most manful struggle going on for fulfilment. I have removed the soil, but I fear too late, the strength of the plants has gone out beneath, and this year there will be no lilies.

JVNE 4,
1894.

www.ingramcontent.com/pod-product-compliance
Lightning Source LLC
Chambersburg PA
CBHW020010030726
47500CB00002B/517